Whose dark or troubled mind will you step into next? Detective or assassin, victim or accomplice? How can you tell reality from delusion when you're spinning in the whirl of a thriller, or trapped in the grip of an unsolvable mystery? When you can't trust your senses, or anyone you meet; that's when you know you're in the hands of the undisputed masters of crime fiction.

Writers of the greatest thrillers and mysteries on earth, who inspired those that followed. Their books are found on shelves all across their home countries—from Asia to Europe, and everywhere in between. Timeless tales that have been devoured, adored and handed down through the decades. Iconic books that have inspired films, and demand to be read and read again. And now we've introduced Pushkin Vertigo Originals—the greatest contemporary crime writing from across the globe, by some of today's best authors.

So step inside a dizzying world of criminal masterminds with **Pushkin Vertigo**. The only trouble you might have is leaving them behind.

FRIEDRICH DÜRRENMATT

PUSHKIN VERTIGO

THE JUDGE AND HIS HANGMAN

Pushkin Press
71–75 Shelton Street
London, WC2H 9JQ

The Judge and His Hangman was first published as *Der Richter und
sein Henker* in *Der Schweizerische Beobachter* 1950/1, and published
in a revised version by Benziger Verlag, Einsiedeln Zurich, 1952

Original text © 1986 by Diogenes Verlag AG Zurich
English translation by Joel Agee © 2006
by Diogenes Verlag AG, Zurich

First published in English by Harper & Row, New York, 1955

First published by Pushkin Press in 2017

1 3 5 7 9 8 6 4 2

9781782273417

Designed and typeset by Tetragon, London

Printed and bound by CPI Group (UK) Ltd, Croydon CRO 4YY

www.pushkinpress.com

THE JUDGE
AND HIS
HANGMAN

1

On the morning of November third, 1948, Alphons Clenin, the policeman of the village of Twann, came upon a blue Mercedes parked by the side of the highway right by the woods where the road from Lamboing comes out of the Twann River gorge. It was one of those foggy mornings of which there were many in that late fall, and Clenin had already walked past the car when he decided to have another look. He had casually glanced through the clouded windows and had the impression that he had seen the driver slumped over the wheel. Being a decent and level-headed fellow, he immediately assumed the man was drunk and decided to give him a helping hand instead of a summons. He would wake him, drive him to Twann, and sober him up with some soup and black coffee at the Bear Inn. For while drunk driving was forbidden by law, drunk sleeping in a stationary car by the side of the road was not forbidden. Clenin opened the door and laid a fatherly hand on the stranger's shoulder. At that moment he noticed that the man was dead. He had been shot through the temples. And now Clenin saw that the door by the passenger seat was unlatched. There was little blood in the car and the dead man's dark-gray coat wasn't even stained. The gleaming edge of a yellow wallet stuck out of the inside pocket. Clenin pulled it out and had no trouble establishing that the dead man was Ulrich Schmied, a police lieutenant from Bern.

Clenin didn't quite know what to do. As a village policeman, he had never had to deal with violence of this magnitude. He paced back and forth by the side of the road. When the rising sun broke through the mist and shone on the corpse, it made him uncomfortable. He went back to the car, picked up the gray felt hat that lay at the dead man's feet, and pulled it down over his head until he could no longer see the pierced temples. Now he felt better.

The policeman again crossed over to the side of the road facing Twann, and wiped the sweat from his forehead. Then he made a decision. He shifted the dead man onto the passenger seat, carefully propped him up, fastened him with a leather strap he found in the back of the car, and sat down behind the wheel.

The motor wouldn't start, but Clenin easily coasted the car down the steep road to Twann and stopped by the gas station in front of the Bear. The attendant never noticed that the distinguished-looking man sitting motionless in the front seat was dead. That was just fine with Clenin. He hated scandals.

But as he drove along the edge of the lake toward Biel, the fog thickened again, the sun disappeared, and the morning turned dark as Judgment Day. Clenin found himself in a long line of cars that for some inexplicable reason were driving even more slowly than the weather required. Almost like a funeral procession, he thought involuntarily. The corpse sat motionless

8

at his side, except for moments when a bump in the road made him nod like an Oriental sage. This made Clenin less and less inclined to pass the cars ahead of him. They reached Biel much later than he had expected.

While the routine investigation of the Schmied case got under way in Biel, the sad facts were conveyed to Inspector Barlach, who had been the dead man's superior in Bern.

Barlach had lived abroad for many years and had made a name for himself as a criminologist, first in Constantinople and later in Germany. His last job there had been as chief of the crime division of the Frankfurt am Main police, but he had come back to his native city as early as 1933. The reason for his return was not his love of Bern—his golden grave, as he often called it—but a slap he had given a high-ranking official of the new German government. This vicious assault was the talk of Frankfurt for a while. Opinions in Bern, always sensitive to the shifts in European politics, judged it first as an inexcusable outrage, then as a deplorable but understandable act, and finally—in 1945—as the only possible thing a Swiss could have done.

Barlach's first action in the Schmied case was to instruct his subordinates to maintain complete secrecy for the first few days—an order which it took all his prestige and authority to enforce. "We know too little," he said, "and besides, newspapers are the most superfluous invention of the last two thousand years."

9

Barlach evidently expected this secret procedure to bring results, in contrast to his "boss," Dr. Lucius Lutz, who lectured in criminology at the university. This official, the son of an ancient Bern family who owed their fortune to the beneficent interference of a rich uncle from Basel, had just returned from a visit to the police departments of New York and Chicago and was "appalled at the antediluvian state of crime prevention in the federal capital of Switzerland," as he publicly stated to Police Commissioner Freiberger on the occasion of a joint ride home in the streetcar.

That same morning, after another call to the Biel police, Barlach paid a visit to the Schönlers, the family in whose house on Bantigerstrasse Schmied had rented a room. As usual, he walked through the old part of town and across the Nydegg bridge, for in his opinion Bern was much too small a city for "streetcars and suchlike."

Climbing the stone steps at Haspelstrasse tired him a little. Moments like this had a way of reminding him that he was over sixty. But soon he found himself at his destination and rang the bell.

It was Frau Schönler herself who opened the door, a short, fat lady not without a certain distinction and dignity. She immediately let Barlach in, for she knew him.

"Schmied had to go away on business last night," Barlach said. "He had to leave quickly, so he asked me to send something on to him. Kindly take me to his room, Frau Schönler."

The lady nodded, and they walked down the hall past a picture in a heavy gold frame. Barlach glanced at it; it was Böcklin's *Island of the Dead*.

"So where is Herr Schmied?" the fat woman asked as she opened the room.

"Abroad," Barlach said, looking up at the ceiling.

The room was on the ground floor, with a view through a doorway onto a small garden planted with old brown fir trees that were apparently sick, for the ground was densely covered with needles. No doubt this was the best room in the house. Barlach went to the desk and looked around once more. One of the dead man's ties lay on the couch.

"He's gone to the tropics, hasn't he, Herr Barlach," Frau Schönler asked, unable to suppress her curiosity.

The question startled him. "No, he's not in the tropics, he's a bit higher up."

Frau Schönler opened her eyes wide and clapped her hands over her head. "My God! In the Himalayas?"

"Close," Barlach said. "You almost guessed it." He opened a folder that was lying on the desk and immediately tucked it under his arm.

"Did you find what you wanted to send Herr Schmied?"

"I did."

He looked around again, avoiding a second glance at the necktie.

"He is the best tenant we have ever had, and there has never been any trouble with lady visitors and such," Frau Schönler assured him.

Barlach went to the door. "I'll send an officer around now and then or come by myself. Schmied has some other important documents that we may need."

"Do you think he'll send me a postcard from abroad?" Frau Schönler wanted to know. "My son collects stamps."

Barlach looked at Frau Schönler with a pensive frown. "It's very unlikely," he said. "Policemen usually don't send postcards when they're traveling on duty. It's not allowed."

Thereupon Frau Schönler again clapped her hands over her head and remarked with exasperation, "The things they forbid nowadays!"

Barlach left and was glad to leave the house behind him.

2

Deeply absorbed in thought, he ate his lunch in the Café du Théâtre instead of his favorite restaurant, the Schmiedstube, leafing through Schmied's folder as he ate and reading some pages with close attention. Then, after a brief walk along the Bundesterrasse, he returned to his office at two o'clock, where he was informed that Schmied's body had arrived from Biel. However, he decided not to pay a visit to his former subordinate. He did not much care for corpses and therefore generally left them in peace. He would have also gladly done without a visit to Lutz, but this one he could not avoid. He carefully locked Schmied's folder in his desk without examining it any further, lit a cigar, and went to Lutz's office, well knowing how Lutz always resented the liberty the old man took by smoking in his room. Only once, years ago, had Lutz dared to object, but Barlach with a dismissive gesture replied that he had served ten years in Turkey and had always smoked in the offices of his superiors in Constantinople, a remark that carried all the more weight in that there was no way to disprove it.

Dr. Lucius Lutz received Barlach nervously, since in his opinion nothing had yet been done, and offered him a comfortable chair near his desk.

"No news from Biel yet?" Barlach asked.

"Nothing yet," Lutz replied.

"I wonder why not," Barlach said. "They're working like crazy." Barlach sat down and glanced at the pictures by Traffelet on the walls, tinted pen-and-ink drawings of soldiers under a large waving flag, sometimes with a general, sometimes without, marching either from left to right or else from right to left.

"It is an alarming," Lutz began, "indeed an increasingly frightening thing to behold the degree to which criminology in this country is still in its infancy. God knows I'm used to inefficiency in our canton, but the procedure that is evidently considered the natural course to take in the case of a murdered police lieutenant casts such an appalling light on the professional competence of our village police that I am still horrified."

"Rest assured, Dr. Lutz," Barlach replied, "our village police are as fit for their job as the police in Chicago, and I'm certain we'll find out who killed Schmied."

"Do you have someone in mind as a suspect, Inspector Barlach?"

Barlach gazed at Lutz for a long time and finally said, "Yes, I have someone in mind, Doctor Lutz."

"Whom?"

"I can't tell you yet."

"Well, that's very interesting," Lutz said, "I know that you are always prepared, Inspector Barlach, to prettify some blunder committed in disregard of modern scientific criminology. But don't forget that time marches on and will not stop for anyone, not even

14

for the most famous criminologist. I have seen crimes in New York and Chicago the likes of which you in our dear old Bern have never imagined. But now a police lieutenant has been murdered, and that is a sure sign that here too, the walls of public security are beginning to crack, and surely that calls for ruthless measures."

"Certainly," Barlach replied, "that is what I am doing."

"Well, I'm glad to hear that," Lutz replied.

A clock was ticking on the wall.

Barlach gingerly pressed his left hand on his belly and with his right hand extinguished his cigar in the ashtray Lutz had set before him. He told Lutz that for some time now he had not been in the best of health, and that his doctor was starting to worry about him. It was stomach trouble, he said, and he would be grateful if Dr. Lutz would appoint someone who could assist him with the legwork in the Schmied murder case, so that Barlach could work from his desk. Lutz agreed. "Whom do you want as your assistant?"

"Tschanz," Barlach said. "He's on vacation in the Bernese Oberland, but we could recall him."

Lutz replied, "Good idea. Tschanz is a man who works hard at keeping up with the latest advances in criminology."

Then he turned his back on Barlach and gazed out the window at the broad expanse of the Waisenhausplatz, which was full of children.

Suddenly he felt an irresistible urge to argue with Barlach about the value of modern scientific criminology. He turned around, but Barlach had already left.

Even though it was close to five already, Barlach decided to drive to the scene of the crime. He took Blatter along, a tall bloated policeman who never spoke a word, whom Barlach liked for that reason, and who also drove the car. In Twann they were welcomed by Clenin, who was looking defiant in anticipation of a reprimand. But the inspector was friendly, shook his hand and said it was a pleasure to meet a man who knew how to think for himself. These words made Clenin proud, though he wasn't quite sure what the old man meant by them. He led Barlach up the road toward the scene of the crime. Blatter lagged behind, disgruntled at having to walk.

Barlach wondered about the name of the town, Lamboing.

"It's Lamlingen in German," Clenin informed him.

"I see," said Barlach. "That sounds much better."

They arrived at the scene of the murder. On their right, the side of the road facing Twann was lined by a wall.

"Where was the car, Clenin?"

"Here," the policeman replied, pointing at the pavement, "almost in the middle of the road," and, since Barlach was hardly paying any attention, "Maybe it would have been better if I had left the car here with the body inside."

"Why?" Barlach asked, looking up at the cliffs of the Jura mountains. "The dead should be removed as quickly as possible, there's no reason why they should stick around. You were right to drive Schmied back to Biel."

Barlach stepped to the edge of the road and looked down over Twann. There was nothing but vineyards between him and the old village. The sun had already set. The road curved like a snake between the houses, and a long freight train stood waiting in the station.

"Didn't anyone hear anything down there, Clenin?" he asked. "The village is nearby. You would hear a shot."

"No one heard anything except the sound of the motor running all night, and no one thought that meant anything bad had happened."

"Of course not, why would they." He looked at the vineyards again. "How is the wine this year, Clenin?"

"Good. We could try some."

"Yes, I would very much like a glass of new wine."

And he struck against something hard with his right foot. He bent down and picked up a small, longish piece of metal flattened in the front, and held it between his thin fingers. Clenin and Blatter leaned in to look at it more closely.

"A bullet," Blatter said. "From a pistol."

"You've done it again, Inspector!" Clenin said admiringly.

"Just a coincidence," Barlach said, and they walked down the road toward Twann.

17

3

Apparently the new wine did not agree with Barlach, for he declared the next morning that he had been throwing up all night. Lutz, who met the inspector on the stairs, was genuinely concerned for his wellbeing and advised him to go the doctor.

"Sure, sure," Barlach mumbled, adding that he liked doctors even less than modern scientific criminology.

Once he was in his office he felt better. He sat down behind his desk, unlocked his drawer, and pulled out the dead man's folder.

At ten o'clock—Barlach was still immersed in his reading—Tschanz came to see him. He had returned from his vacation late the previous night.

Barlach started at the sight of him. For a moment it had seemed as if the dead Schmied had come into the room. Tschanz was wearing the same coat as Schmied's and a similar felt hat. Only the round and good-natured face was different.

"Good thing you're here, Tschanz," Barlach said. "We have to discuss the Schmied case. You'll have to take over most of the job, I'm not well."

"Yes, I've already heard," said Tschanz.

Tschanz pulled up a chair and sat down, resting his left arm on Barlach's desk. Schmied's folder was lying open on the desk.

Barlach leaned back in his chair. "To you I can speak frankly," he began. "I've come across thousands of policemen, good ones and bad ones, between Constantinople and Bern. Many were no better than the poor bastards we populate the jails with, except that they happen to be on the other side of the law. But Schmied was in a class of his own, he had real talent. He could have put us all in his pocket. He had a clear mind, he knew what he wanted, and he kept it to himself. He spoke only when it was necessary. We have to emulate him, Tschanz, he was way ahead of us."

Tschanz slowly turned his head toward Barlach, for he had been looking out the window, and said, "That could be."

Barlach saw that he was not convinced.

"We don't know much about his death," the inspector continued, "this bullet is all we've got." And he told him where he had found the bullet, and placed it on the desk. Tschanz picked it up and looked at it.

"It's from an army pistol," he said, and returned the bullet.

Barlach closed the folder on his desk. "Above all, we don't know what Schmied was doing in Twann or Lamlingen. He never had an assignment to the Lake Biel area, I would have known about that. We don't have even a remotely probable motive for his driving out there."

Tschanz, who was only half listening to what Barlach was saying, crossed his legs and said, "All we know is how Schmied was murdered."

"And how would you know that?" the inspector asked, not without surprise, after a pause.

"The steering wheel on Schmied's car is on the left, and you found the bullet on the left side of the road, as seen from the car; and the people in Twann heard the motor running all night. Schmied was stopped by the killer as he was driving from Lamboing to Twann. He probably knew the killer, otherwise he wouldn't have stopped. Schmied opened the door on the right to let the killer in and sat back behind the wheel. At that moment he was shot. Schmied must have been unaware that the man intended to kill him."

Barlach considered this interpretation. Then he said, "Now I'll have a cigar after all," and then, after lighting it, "You are right, Tschanz, that's more or less what must have happened, I'm willing to believe that. But this still doesn't explain what Schmied was doing on the road between Twann and Lamlingen."

Tschanz pointed out that Schmied had been wearing evening clothes under his overcoat.

"He did? I didn't know that," Barlach said.

"But haven't you seen the body?"

"No, I don't like corpses."

"But it was in the official record."

"I like official records even less."

Tschanz said nothing.

But Barlach remarked, "This just makes the case more complicated. What was Schmied doing wearing a tuxedo by the Twann River gorge?"

"On the contrary," Tschanz replied, "it could simplify the case. I'm sure there aren't many people around Lamboing who are rich enough to give black tie parties."

He drew out a small pocket calendar and explained that it had belonged to Schmied.

"I've seen it," Barlach nodded. "There's nothing in it of any importance."

Tschanz contradicted him. "For Wednesday, November second, Schmied had entered a G. It was on that day that he was killed, shortly before midnight, according to the coroner. Then there's another G on Wednesday the twenty-sixth, and again on Tuesday, October eighteenth."

"G could mean all sorts of things," Barlach said. "A woman's name, or anything."

"Hardly a woman's name," Tschanz replied. "Schmied's fiancée's name is Anna, and Schmied was a steady sort of guy."

"I don't know about her either," the inspector admitted; and seeing that Tschanz was surprised at his ignorance, he said, "All I'm interested in, Tschanz, is who killed Schmied."

"Of course," Tschanz replied politely. But then he shook his head and laughed, "You're a strange man, Inspector."

"I'm an old black tomcat who likes to eat mice." Barlach said this very seriously.

Tschanz didn't know what to say to that. Finally he replied, "On the days he marked with a G, Schmied put on his tuxedo and drove off in his Mercedes."

"Now how do you know that?"

"From Frau Schönler."

"I see," Barlach said and fell silent. But then he said, "Yes, these are facts."

Tschanz looked keenly into the commissioner's face, lit a cigarette, and said with some hesitation, "Dr. Lutz told me you have a definite suspicion."

"Yes, Tschanz, I do."

"Commissioner, since I have become your assistant in the Schmied murder case, don't you think it might be better if you told me who it is you're suspecting?"

"You see," Barlach answered slowly, deliberating each word as carefully as Tschanz did, "my suspicion is not a scientific criminological suspicion. I have no solid reasons to justify it. You have seen how little I know. All I have is an idea as to who the murderer might be; but the person I have in mind has yet to deliver the proof of his guilt."

"What do you mean, Inspector?" Tschanz asked.

Barlach smiled. "Simply that I have to wait for the evidence to emerge that will justify his arrest."

"If I am to work with you, I have to know who it is I'm targeting with my investigation," Tschanz declared politely.

"Above all we must remain objective. That applies to me, as the one who holds a suspicion, and to you, as the one who will conduct most of the inquest. I don't know whether my suspicion will be confirmed. I await the results of your investigation. It is your job to find Schmied's killer regardless of my suspicion. If the person I suspect is in fact the killer, you will find him in your own way—which, unlike mine, is impeccably scientific. And if I'm wrong, you will find the right man, and there will have been no need to know the name of the person I falsely suspected."

They were silent for a while, and then the old man asked, "Are you willing to work with me on this basis?"

Tschanz hesitated a moment before he replied, "All right, I agree."

"What do you want to do now, Tschanz?"

Tschanz walked over to the window. "There's a G on today's date in Schmied's calendar. I want to drive to Lamboing and see what I can find out. I'll leave at seven, the same time Schmied always left when he drove out there."

He turned around again and asked politely, but as if in jest, "Are you coming along, Inspector?"

"Yes, Tschanz, I'm coming along," was the unexpected reply.

"Very well," Tschanz said, a little bewildered, "seven o'clock."

In the doorway he turned around again. "You, too, paid Frau Schönler a visit, Inspector Barlach. Didn't you find anything there?" The old man did not answer right away. First he locked the folder in the drawer of his desk and put the key in his pocket.

"No, Tschanz," he finally said, "I found nothing. You may go now."

4

At seven o'clock Tschanz drove to the riverside house in the Altenberg district where Inspector Barlach had lived since 1933. It was raining, and the speeding police car skidded in the curve by the Nydegg Bridge. But Tschanz quickly regained control. He drove slowly along the Altenbergstrasse, for he had never visited Barlach before, and he peered through the wet windows searching for the house number, which he deciphered with difficulty. He honked the horn several times; there was no sign of any movement inside. Tschanz left the car and hurried through the rain to the door. After a moment of hesitation he pressed down the door handle, since he couldn't see the bell in the dark. The door was open, and Tschanz stepped into a vestibule. He found himself facing a half-open door through which light fell into the hallway. He approached the door, knocked, and, receiving no answer, pushed it open. In front of him was a large room, its walls lined with books. Barlach was lying on a couch. The inspector was asleep, but he seemed prepared for the drive to Lake Biel, for he had his winter coat on. He was holding a book. The sound of Barlach's quiet breathing, the many books on their shelves, filled Tschanz with a deep unease. He looked around cautiously. The room had no windows, but each wall had a door that must lead to other rooms. In the middle of the floor stood a large desk, and on top of it—startling Tschanz the moment he saw it—lay a large brass snake.

"I brought that with me from Constantinople," said a quiet voice from the sofa, and Barlach sat up.

"You see, Tschanz, I already have my coat on. We can leave."

"Pardon me," Tschanz replied, still taken aback, "you were asleep and didn't hear me knocking. I couldn't find the bell."

"I don't have a bell. I don't need one; the door is never locked."

"Not even when you're out?"

"Not even when I'm out. It's always exciting to come home and see whether something's been stolen or not."

Tschanz laughed and picked up the snake from Constantinople. "I was almost killed with that thing once," the inspector remarked somewhat sardonically, and only now did Tschanz notice that the snake's head could be used as a handle and that its body was as sharp as the blade of a knife. Baffled, he looked at the strange glittering ornaments on the terrible weapon. Barlach stood next to him.

"Be ye wise as serpents," he said, giving Tschanz a long and thoughtful look. Then he smiled, "And harmless as doves." And he tapped Tschanz lightly on the shoulder. "I've had some sleep, for the first time in days. Damned stomach."

"It's that bad?" Tschanz asked.

"It's that bad," the inspector coolly replied.

"You should stay home, Herr Barlach, it's cold outside and it's raining."

Barlach looked at Tschanz again and laughed, "Nonsense, there's a killer to be caught. It would suit you just fine if I stayed home, wouldn't it?"

As they were driving across the Nydegg Bridge, Barlach asked, "Why don't you go by way of Aargauerstalden in the direction of Zollikofen, Tschanz? Isn't that quicker than going through the city?"

"Because I don't want to go to Twann via Zollikofen and Biel. I prefer to go via Kerzers and Erlach."

"That is an unusual route, Tschanz."

"It's not so unusual at all, Inspector."

They fell silent. The lights of the city glided past. But when they reached Bethlehem, Tschanz asked, "Did you ever drive with Schmied?"

"Yes, frequently. He was a careful driver." And Barlach cast a pensive glance at the speedometer, which showed almost a hundred and ten kilometers an hour.

Tschanz slowed down a little. "I remember driving with Schmied once, he was slow as hell, and he had a strange sort of name for his car. He used it when he had to stop for gas. Do you remember the name? I forgot it."

"He called his car the Blue Charon," Barlach replied.

"Charon is a name in Greek mythology, right?"

"Charon was the ferryman who took the dead to the underworld, Tschanz."

"Schmied had rich parents, so he got the kind of schooling people like us can't afford. That's why he knew about Charon and we don't."

Barlach put his hands in his coat pockets and looked at the speedometer again. "Yes, Tschanz," he said. "Schmied was well educated, he knew Greek and Latin, and with his college credits he had a great future, but nevertheless I wouldn't go over a hundred."

A little past Gummenen, the car pulled up sharply at a gas station. A man stepped out to attend them.

"Police," Tschanz said. "We need some information."

Indistinctly they saw a curious and somewhat alarmed face peering into the car.

"Do you remember a driver stopping here two days ago who called his car the blue Charon?"

The man shook his head in wonderment, and Tschanz drove on. "We'll ask the next one."

At the gas station in Kerzers, the attendant didn't know anything either.

Barlach grumbled, "This doesn't make any sense."

At Erlach Tschanz was lucky. On Wednesday evening someone like that had stopped for gas, he was told.

"You see," Tschanz said as they turned into the Neuenburg–Biel highway, "now we know that on Wednesday evening Schmied drove through Kerzers and Erlach."

"Are you sure?" asked the inspector.

"I just proved it to you."

"Yes, it's perfectly proven. But what good will it do you, Tschanz?"

"It just is what it is. Every bit of knowledge helps."

"There you're right again," said the old man, looking out for Lake Biel. It was no longer raining. They had just passed Neuveville when the lake emerged among shreds of mist. They drove into Ligerz. Tschanz drove slowly, looking for the exit to Lamboing.

Now the car was climbing through the vineyards. Barlach opened the window and looked down at the lake. A few stars shone above Peters Island. The lights were reflected in the water, and a motorboat was racing across the lake. Late for this time of year, Barlach thought. Down in the valley before them lay Twann and behind them Ligerz.

They went around a curve and drove toward the woods, whose presence they sensed somewhere ahead of them in the night. Tschanz seemed a little unsure and wondered whether this might not be the road to Schernelz. When a man came walking toward them, he stopped. "Is this the way to Lamboing?"

"Just keep going and turn right by the white row of houses, straight into the forest." The man was wearing a leather jacket. He whistled to a small white dog with a black head that was skipping about in front of the headlights.

"Come along, Ping-Ping!"

They left the vineyards behind and were soon in the forest. The fir trees advanced toward them, endless columns in the light. The street was narrow and in

28

need of repair. Every once in a while a branch slapped against the windows. To their right, the cliffs dropped off precipitously. Tschanz drove so slowly that they could hear the sound of rushing water far below.

"The Twann River gorge," Tschanz explained. "On the other side is the road to Twann."

On and off, on their left, white cliffs flashed into view, rising steeply into the night. For the rest, it was very dark, since the moon was still new. Now the road leveled out and the stream was gurgling beside them. They turned left and drove over a bridge. Before them lay a highway—the road from Twann to Lamboing. Tschanz stopped the car.

He turned off the headlights. They were in complete darkness.

"Now what?" asked Barlach.

"Now we'll wait. It's twenty to eight."

5

As they sat there waiting and it turned eight o'clock without anything happening, Barlach said it was time he learned what precisely Tschanz had in mind.

"Nothing precise, Inspector. I haven't gotten that far in the Schmied case, and you're groping in the dark too, even though you have a hunch. Right now I'm staking everything on the possibility that there'll be another party at the same house Schmied went to on Wednesday, and that a few people will come driving past on their way there. A black-tie party nowadays is bound to be a sizable affair. Of course that's just an assumption, Inspector Barlach, but in our profession, that's what assumptions are for: we test them."

The inspector interrupted his subordinate's train of thought with a skeptical objection. "The police in Biel, Neuenstadt, Twann, and Lamlingen have looked into this question of why Schmied came to this area. All their investigations have turned up nothing at all."

"Obviously Schmied's killer was smarter than the police in Biel and Neuenstadt," Tschanz said.

"How would you know that?" Barlach muttered.

"I don't suspect anyone in particular," Tschanz said. "But I do feel respect for whoever it is that killed Schmied. If I may use such a word in this connection."

Barlach listened without moving, his shoulders slightly hunched.

"And you think you'll catch this man, Tschanz, for whom you feel such respect?"

"I hope so, Inspector."

They sat in silence again and waited. Then a glow appeared in the woods near Twann. A pair of headlights glared at them. A car drove past in the direction of Lamboing and vanished into the night.

Tschanz started the motor. Two other cars passed, large dark limousines full of people. Tschanz followed them.

The woods came to an end. They drove past a restaurant with a sign that stood in the light of an open doorway, past farm houses, the glow of the last car's taillight always before them.

They reached the wide plain of the Tessenberg. The sky was swept clean, and huge presences stood in the blackness: Vega descending, Capella rising, Aldebaran, Jupiter's radiant flame.

The road turned north, they saw the outlines of mountains, the Spitzberg, the Chasseral, at their feet a few flickering lights. Those were the villages of Lamboing, Diesse, and Noids.

At that moment the cars ahead of them turned left into a dirt road, and Tschanz stopped. He rolled down his window to stick his head out. They could see the dim contours of a house standing in a field, framed by poplars, its doorway lit up, the three cars stopping in front of it. The sound of voices reached them, then everyone poured into the house and all was still. The light in the doorway went out. "They're not expecting anyone else," Tschanz said.

Barlach got out and breathed the cold night air. It felt good. He watched Tschanz park the car halfway onto the right shoulder of the road, for the street to Lamboing was narrow. Now Tschanz got out and joined the inspector. They walked down the dirt road toward the house on the field. The ground was loamy and puddles had gathered, for it had rained here too.

Then they came to a low wall with a tall, rusty iron gate set into it. The gate was closed. They looked at the house across the wall. The garden was bare, and the limousines lay among the poplars like large animals; there were no lights to be seen. Everything made a desolate impression.

It took them a while before they made out a sign attached to the middle of the gate; it was hanging at an angle. Tschanz turned on the flashlight he had brought from the car: on the sign was a capital G.

They stood in the dark again. "You see," Tschanz said, "my assumption was right. A shot in the dark, and I hit the bull's eye." And then, satisfied:

"How about a cigar, Inspector? I think I deserve one."

Barlach offered him one. "Now all we need to find out is what G stands for."

"That's no problem: Gastmann."

"How so?"

"I looked it up in the telephone book. There are only two G's in Lamboing."

Barlach let out a startled laugh, but then he said: "Couldn't it be the other G?"

"No, that's the Gendarmerie. Or do you think a gendarme had something to do with the murder?"

"Everything's possible, Tschanz," replied the old man.

And Tschanz struck a match, but in the strong wind that was suddenly shaking the poplars as if in a rage, he found it difficult to light his cigar.

6

"I cannot understand," Barlach said, "how the police of Lamboing, Diesse, and Lignières managed to overlook this Gastmann. His house isn't exactly hidden, it's easily visible from Lamboing, in fact it would be impossible to hold a large party here without the whole village knowing about it."

Tschanz replied that he could not explain this yet either.

Thereupon they decided to walk around the house. They separated; each took a different side.

Tschanz vanished into the night and Barlach was alone. He went to the right. He turned up the collar of his coat, for it was cold. One again he felt the heavy pressure on his stomach, the violent stabs of pain, and there was a cold sweat on his forehead. He walked along the wall and followed its turn to the left. The house still lay in complete blackness.

He stopped and leaned against the wall. He saw the lights of Lamboing by the edge of the forest. Then he walked on. Again the wall changed direction, this time toward the west. The back of the house was lit up, and bright light poured through a row of windows on the second floor. He heard the sound of a piano, and when he listened more closely, he noticed that someone was playing Bach.

He walked on. According to his calculations he

was about to meet Tschanz. He strenuously peered across the brightly lit lawn, and realized too late that a dog was standing a few steps away from him. Barlach knew a lot about dogs, but he had never seen one this size before. Though he could distinguish no details but only recognized the silhouette set off against the lighter surface of the lawn, the beast seemed to be of such terrifying proportions that Barlach instinctively froze. He saw the massive head turn slowly, as if accidentally, and stare at him. Its round eyes were bright, empty disks.

The unexpectedness of the encounter, the massive size of the animal, and the strangeness of its appearance paralyzed him. He retained the coolness of his reason, but he forgot the need for action. He looked at the beast, unafraid but captivated. This was how evil had always drawn him into its spell, the great riddle that lured him again and again to attempt a solution.

And as the dog suddenly leaped at him, a monstrous shadow hurtling through the air, a creature of pure raving murderous power, tearing him to the ground with such speed that he barely had time to raise his left arm to protect his throat, the old man did not utter a cry or so much as a sound, so natural did it all seem to him and in keeping with the laws of this world.

But just before the beast could crush the arm it had gripped with its fangs, Barlach heard the whip-crack of a shot; the body on top of him jerked, and warm blood poured onto his hand. The dog was dead.

The weight of the inert body pressed down on him, and Barlach stroked it with his hand, feeling a smooth and sweaty hide. Trembling and with an effort, he stood up, wiped his hand on the sparse grass. Tschanz came up to him, tucking the revolver back in his coat pocket as he approached.

"Are you all right, Inspector?" he asked, looking with concern at Barlach's torn sleeve.

"Absolutely. He didn't have time to bite through."

Tschanz crouched down and turned the animal's head toward the light, which was refracted in the dead eyes.

"Fangs like a wolf," he said, with a shiver. "He would have torn you to pieces, Inspector."

"You saved my life, Tschanz."

"Don't you ever carry a gun, sir?"

Barlach touched the motionless mass with his foot. "Very rarely, Tschanz," he replied, and they fell silent.

The dead dog lay on the bare, dirty ground, and they looked down at it. At their feet, a large black pool had formed—it was the blood flowing from the beast's throat like a dark lava stream.

When they looked up again, the scene had changed. The music had stopped, the lighted windows had been thrown open, and people in evening clothes were leaning out. Barlach and Tschanz looked at each other, embarrassed at finding themselves arraigned before a tribunal, as it were, and in this godforsaken spot of all places—where the fox and the hare bid each other good night, as the inspector said to himself in his annoyance.

In the middle one of the five windows stood a single man, separate from the others, who called out in a strange and clear voice, asking what they were doing down there.

"Police," Barlach replied quietly, adding that they needed to speak to Herr Gastmann.

The man replied that he thought it peculiar that they should have to kill a dog in order to meet Herr Gastmann; and besides, he was in the mood to listen to Bach. Whereupon he shut the window again, with a motion that was like his manner of speaking: unhurried, deliberate, and supremely indifferent.

A flurry of exclamations came from the windows: "Disgraceful!" "What do you think, Herr Direktor?" "Scandalous," "Unbelievable, the way the police carry on." Then the people withdrew, one window after another was shut, and all was quiet.

The two policemen had no choice but to retrace their steps. At the entrance gate, on the front side of the garden wall, a solitary figure was pacing back and forth in great agitation.

"Quick, flash your light on him," Barlach whispered at Tschanz, and in the beam of the flashlight they saw above an elegant suit and tie a rather bloated face, with features that were not undistinguished but blunted by dissipation. A heavy ring glittered on one of his hands. Upon a whispered word from Barlach, the light was switched off again.

"Who in the hell are you, fellow?" the fat man growled.

"Inspector Barlach—are you Herr Gastmann?"

"State Councillor von Schwendi, fellow, also known as Colonel von Schwendi. Good God in heaven, who do you think you are, banging around like that?"

"We are conducting an investigation and need to speak to Herr Gastmann, State Councillor," Barlach replied calmly.

The state councillor refused to be so easily appeased. "You're a separatist, aren't you?" he thundered.

Barlach decided to address him by his other title and cautiously suggested that the colonel was mistaken, this had nothing to do with the Jura problem.

But before Barlach could continue, the colonel became even more incensed than the state councillor. "So you're a communist! To hell with the lot of you! We're having a private concert here, so take your target practice somewhere else! As a colonel, I will not put up with any demonstrations against Western civilization! I will have order restored, with the Swiss Army if need be!"

Since the state councillor was evidently confused, Barlach was forced to enlighten him.

"Tschanz, don't put the state councillor's remarks in your report," he said in a dryly officious tone.

The state councillor instantly regained his composure.

"What sort of report, fellow?"

As inspector of the Criminal Investigation Department of the Bern Police, Barlach explained, he had to conduct an investigation of the murder of Police Lieutenant Schmied. It was his duty, he said, to keep a record of everything that certain persons may have to say in reply to his questions, but since . . .—and again he hesitated, unsure which of the man's two titles to use—since the colonel had evidently misconstrued the situation, he would not record the state councillor's words in his report.

The colonel was taken aback.

"So you're with the police," he said. "That's another matter."

He begged their pardon. He had an awfully full day behind him, lunch at the Turkish embassy, in the afternoon he had been elected president of an officers' club, the "Swiss Swords," then he had to attend a celebration of his election at the Helvetian Society, and earlier in the morning a special meeting of his political party, and now this get-together at Gastmann's to hear a pianist, a world-famous one, true, but still, he was dead tired.

"Isn't it possible to speak to Herr Gastmann?" Barlach asked again.

"What do you want of Gastmann?" von Schwendi replied. "What does he have to do with a murdered police lieutenant?"

"Schmied visited him last Wednesday and was killed on his way home near Twann."

"That's what you get," the state councillor said. "Gastmann invites anyone and everyone, no wonder it ends up with an incident."

Then he fell silent and appeared to be thinking.

"I am Gastmann's lawyer," he finally said. "Why did you come on this particular night? You could have at least called beforehand."

Barlach explained that he and his colleague had only just discovered Gastmann's part in the case.

The colonel was still not satisfied.

"And what about the dog?"

"He attacked me, and Tschanz had to shoot."

"Well, that's all right then," von Schwendi said, not without friendliness. "You really can't speak to Gastmann tonight. Even the police occasionally have to respect other people's social obligations. I'll have a quick word with Gastmann tonight, and I'll be in your office tomorrow. Do you happen to have a picture of Schmied?"

Barlach took a photograph from his wallet and gave it to him.

"Thank you," the state councillor said.

Then he nodded and went inside.

Now Barlach and Tschanz walked back to where they had stood earlier, in front of the rusty bars of the garden gate; the front of the house was still dark.

"You can't get past a state councillor," Barlach said, "and if he's a colonel and a lawyer on top of it, he's got three devils inside him at once. So here we are with our lovely murder, and there's nothing we can do."

Tschanz was silent and seemed to be pondering something. Finally he said, "It is nine o'clock, Inspector. I think the best thing we can do is look up the policeman of Lamboing and find out what he knows about Gastmann."

"Right," Barlach said. "You can do that. Try to find out why no one in Lamboing knows anything about Schmied's visiting Gastmann. I'm going to that little restaurant at the edge of the gorge. I have to do something for my stomach. I'll expect you there."

They walked back along the path to the car. Tschanz drove off and reached Lamboing after a few minutes.

He found the policeman in the inn, together with Clenin, who had come up from Twann. They were sitting at a table apart from the farmers. Evidently they had something private to discuss. The policeman of Lamboing was short, fat, and red-haired. His name was Jean Pierre Charnel.

Tschanz joined them, and soon the suspicion the two men felt for their colleague from Bern was dissipated, although Charnel minded having to switch from French to German, a language in which he felt himself on slippery ground. They were drinking white wine, and Tschanz ate some bread and cheese with it. He did not mention that he had just come from Gastmann's house, but asked instead if they still had not found any clues.

"*Non*," said Charnel, "not a trace of *assassin. On a rien trouvé*, nothing was found."

Charnel went on to say that in this area there was only one person worth questioning, a Herr Gastmann, the one who had bought Rollier's house, where there were always a lot of guests, and on Wednesday he'd had a big party. But Schmied hadn't been there, Gastmann didn't even know his name. "*Schmied n'etait pas chez Gastmann, impossible.* Completely impossible."

41

Tschanz listened to the man's garbled talk and suggested questioning some other people who had been at Gastmann's on that day.

"I've done that," Clenin interjected. "There's a writer in Schernelz, above Ligerz, who knows Gastmann well and visits him often. He says he was there on Wednesday. He doesn't know anything about Schmied, never heard his name, and he doesn't believe Gastmann ever had a policeman in his house."

"A writer, you say?" Tschanz frowned. "I'll have to buttonhole that one some time. Writers are a two-faced bunch, but I know how to handle a smart-ass."

"So tell me, Charnel," he continued, "who is this Gastmann?"

"*Un monsieur très riche*," the policeman of Lamboing replied enthusiastically. "Has money like hay and *très noble*. He give tip to my *fiancée*"—and he pointed proudly at the waitress—"*comme un roi*, but not on purpose to have something with her. *Jamais.*"

"What's his profession?"

"*Philosophe.*"

"What does that mean to you, Charnel?"

"A man who think much and do nothing."

"But he must make money somehow?"

Charnel shook his head. "He do not make money, he have money. He pay taxes for the whole village of Lamboing. That is enough for us to make Gastmann the man most *sympathique* in the whole canton."

"We'll still have to have a close look at this Gastmann. I'm going to see him tomorrow."

"Watch out for his dog," Charnel warned. *"Un chien très dangereux."*

Tschanz stood up and patted the policeman of Lamboing on the shoulder. "Don't worry, I can handle his dog."

7

It was ten o'clock when Tschanz left Clenin and Charnel to join Barlach in the restaurant by the ravine. But when he came to the spot where the dirt road branched off to Gastmann's house, he stopped his car. He got out and slowly walked to the garden gate and then along the wall. The house still looked dark and solitary, surrounded by giant poplars swaying in the wind. The limousines were still parked in the garden. Tschanz did not go all the way around the house, but stopped at a corner from which he could survey the lighted windows in the back. Now and then the shapes of people were silhouetted against the yellow panes, and Tschanz pressed himself close to the wall to avoid being seen. He scanned the sparse patch of lawn where the dog had lain. It was no longer there. Someone must have removed it. Only the black pool of blood still glinted in the light from the windows. Tschanz returned to the car.

Barlach was not in the restaurant when he got there. The proprietress said he had left for Twann half an hour ago, after drinking a brandy—he hadn't stayed more than five minutes.

Tschanz wondered what the old man was up to, but he was unable to pursue his speculations; the narrow road demanded all his attention. He drove past the bridge where they had waited, and drove on into the forest.

And now something strange and uncanny occurred that put him in a pensive mood. He had been driving quickly when suddenly the lake flashed into view from below, a nocturnal mirror framed by white cliffs. He realized he had reached the scene of the murder. At that moment, a dark figure detached itself from the wall of rock and clearly signaled for the car to stop.

Tschanz halted automatically and opened the right-hand door of the car. He regretted this immediately, for he realized that he was going through precisely the same motions Schmied had just moments before he was shot. He thrust his hand in his coat pocket and gripped his revolver. The touch of its cool steel calmed him. The figure came closer. Then he recognized who it was: Barlach. But far from relieving him, this realization filled him with a hot, secret terror that he could not explain to himself. Barlach stooped and they looked each other in the face—for hours, it seemed, though it was only a few seconds. Neither of them said a word, and their eyes were like stones. Then Barlach got into the car, and Tschanz released his grip on the gun in his pocket.

"You can drive on, Tschanz," Barlach said, and his voice sounded indifferent. But Tschanz noticed with a start that the old man had addressed him with "*du*" instead of the formal "*Sie*." From then on, the inspector persisted in this more intimate form of address.

Not until they passed Biel did Barlach break the silence and ask what Tschanz had experienced in

Lamboing, "and let's settle once and for all on calling the place by its French name."

When Tschanz told him that both Charnel and Clenin thought it impossible that Schmied had been a guest at Gastmann's, Barlach said nothing; and as for the writer from Schernelz whom Clenin had mentioned, Barlach said he would speak to the man himself.

Tschanz spoke with more animation than usual. He was relieved that they were talking at all, and he wanted to drown out the strange agitation he felt, but before they reached Schupfen, they were both silent again.

Shortly after eleven, they stopped in front of Barlach's house, and the inspector got out.

"Thanks again, Tschanz," he said, and shook his hand. "It's an embarrassing thing to talk about: but the fact is, you saved my life."

He stood on the pavement and followed the vanishing taillight of the speeding car. "Now he can drive as fast as he likes."

He entered his house by the unlocked door. In the book-lined hallway he put his hand in his coat pocket and pulled out a weapon, which he carefully placed on the desk next to the snake. It was a large, heavy revolver.

Then he slowly took off his overcoat. Wrapped around his left arm was a thick cloth bandage, the kind animal trainers use to teach a dog to attack.

8

The next morning, the old inspector knew from experience that some "unpleasantness"—his word for friction with Lutz—was to be expected. "You know what Saturdays are like," he told himself as he crossed the Altenberg bridge. "That's when the bureaucrats bare their teeth just because they're ashamed of not having done anything sensible the whole week." He was dressed in solemn black, for Schmied's funeral was scheduled for ten o'clock. There was no way he could avoid attending it, and that was the real source of his irritation.

Von Schwendi appeared at police headquarters shortly after eight, bypassing Barlach and instead going to Lutz, who had just received Tschanz's report about the previous night's events.

Von Schwendi was in the same political faction as Lutz, the conservative liberal-socialist wing of the Independent Party. He had actively lobbied for Lutz's advancement, and ever since a tête-à-tête over dinner following a closed session of the executive committee, Lutz and von Schwendi had been on "*du*" terms, even though Lutz had not been elected to the local parliament seat; for in Bern, as von Schwendi explained, it is practically impossible for a man with the first name of Lucius to become a people's representative.

"It's really something," he began the moment his bulky shape appeared in the doorway, "the way your people from the Bern police carry on, my dear Lutz. They shoot my client Gastmann's dog, a rare South American breed, and disrupt culture—Anatol Kraushaar-Raffaeli, a world-famous pianist. Let's face it: the Swiss have no education, no cosmopolitan character, not a trace of European consciousness. There's only one remedy: three years of military service."

Lutz, who found the visit of his political associate embarrassing, and who was afraid of his endless tirades, offered von Schwendi a seat.

"We are embroiled in an extremely difficult investigation," he said, intimidated. "You know it yourself, and the young policeman who is conducting it for the main part is, by Swiss standards, rather good at his job. The old inspector who was with him is, admittedly, somewhat rusty. I regret the death of such a rare South American dog. I'm an animal lover and own a dog myself, and I will order a special, thorough investigation. Our men just haven't the faintest inkling of real criminology. When I think of Chicago, I find our situation downright hopeless."

Lutz paused, unsettled by von Schwendi's unblinking stare, and by the time he resumed speaking, he felt profoundly unsure of himself.

"I would like to know," he said, "whether the murdered man, Schmied, was a guest at your client's house last Wednesday evening. You see, we have some reason to believe that he was."

"My dear Lutz," the colonel replied, "let's not play

games here. You people know all about Schmied's visits to Gastmann, you can't fool me."

"What do you mean by that, State Councillor?" In his bewilderment, Lutz reverted to the formal address. He had never felt quite at ease conversing with von Schwendi on a "*du*" basis.

The lawyer leaned back, folded his hands in front of his chest, and bared his teeth, a pose that had contributed substantially to his attaining his colonel's rank as well as his state councillor's title.

"My dear doctor," he said, "I'd really like to know once and for all why you people had this Schmied fellow sniffing around good old Gastmann. Because whatever is going on out there in the Jura Mountains, it's none of the police's damn business, we don't have a Gestapo here, not yet at any rate."

Lutz was flabbergasted. "Why on earth would we have Schmied investigate your client, who is completely unknown to us?" he asked helplessly. "And why should a murder be none of our business?"

"If you don't know that Schmied attended Gastmann's parties in Lamboing under the name of Doctor Prantl, lecturer on American Cultural History in München, then the entire police force should resign for reasons of total incompetence." Agitated, von Schwendi drummed his fingers on Lutz's desk.

"My dear Oscar, we don't know anything about it," Lutz said, relieved to have finally remembered the state councillor's first name. "What you are telling me is real news to me."

"Aha," von Schwendi said dryly, and lapsed into silence. Lutz was becoming more and more conscious of his inferiority. Sensing that he would have to yield step by step to whatever the colonel might require of him, he helplessly glanced at the Traffelets on the wall, at the marching soldiers, the fluttering Swiss flags, the general on his horse. The state councillor noted the police chief's embarrassment with satisfaction and decided to clarify the caustic meaning of his "Aha."

"So it's news to the police," he said. "Once again the police know nothing at all."

Even though confessing it was extremely unpleasant, and though von Schwendi's bullying was very nearly intolerable, the police chief was forced to admit that Schmied had not visited Gastmann on official assignment, that the police had in fact been ignorant of his trips to Lamboing. "Evidently," he said, "Schmied was acting purely on his own. As for why he would assume a false name—I cannot at present explain this either."

Von Schwendi bent forward and fixed his bloodshot, watery eyes on Lutz. "That explains everything," he said. "Schmied was spying for a foreign power."

"What do you mean?" By now Lutz was floundering more than ever.

"What I mean," said the state councillor, "is that the police must find out Schmied's motives for visiting Gastmann."

"The police, my dear Oscar, should first and above all find out some things about Gastmann," said Lutz.

50

"Gastmann is no threat to the police," von Schwendi retorted, "and besides I don't want you or anyone from the police to concern yourselves with him. That is his wish, he is my client, and it's my duty to see that his wishes are complied with."

This insolent reply had such a shattering effect on Lutz that at first he was unable to formulate a response. He lit a cigarette, forgetting in his confusion to offer one to von Schwendi. Then he finally shifted his position in his chair and replied:

"Unfortunately, the fact that Schmied visited Gastmann forces us to concern ourselves with your client, my dear Oscar."

Von Schwendi would not be deterred. "Not so much with my client," he said, "but mainly with me, since I am Gastmann's lawyer. It's your good fortune, Lutz, that you have me to deal with, because frankly, I want to help you as well as Gastmann. Naturally, the whole case is disagreeable for my client, but I dare say it's even more embarrassing for you, since the police are still groping in the dark. And frankly, I doubt whether you'll ever be able to cast any light on this affair."

"The police," Lutz replied, "have solved almost every murder, that is a statistically proven fact. I admit that in the Schmied case we've run into certain difficulties, but we have also"—he hesitated for a moment—"arrived at some remarkable results. It's we, after all, who discovered the Gastmann connection, and it's again because of our actions that Gastmann has sent you to us. It's up to Gastmann

51

now to explain his connection to Schmied, it's his problem, not ours. Schmied was in his house, under a false identity, true, but that is precisely the reason why the police are obliged to concern themselves with Gastmann, for surely the murdered man's peculiar behavior does implicate Gastmann. We must have a talk with Gastmann. Unless, of course, you can furnish a satisfactory explanation as to why Schmied visited your client under a false name, not just once but several times, according to our findings."

"All right," von Schwendi said. "Let's get down to brass tacks. You will see in due course that it's you and not I who will have to furnish a satisfactory explanation as to what Gastmann was after in Lamboing. It's you, the police, who are in the dock here, not we, my dear Lutz."

With these words he pulled out of his briefcase a large white sheet of paper, unfolded it, and laid it on the police chief's desk.

"These are the names of the persons who have been guests at Gastmann's house," he said. "The list is complete. I have divided it into three sections. The first we'll ignore, it's irrelevant, those are the artists. No offense against Kraushaar-Raffaeli, he's a foreigner; no, I mean the local types, the ones from Utzendorf and Merlingen. They either write plays about Niklaus Manuel and the battle of Morgarten or else it's one mountain landscape after another. The second section are the industrialists. You'll see the names, they have a proud ring to them, these are men whom I regard

52

as the finest representatives of Swiss society. I say this quite openly, even though I myself come from peasant stock on my maternal grandmother's side."

"And the third section?" asked Lutz, since the state councillor had suddenly stopped talking. Von Schwendi's calm made the police chief nervous, which of course was his intention.

"The third section," von Schwendi finally continued, "makes the Schmied affair unpleasant for you and also, I have to admit this, for the industrialists; because now I am compelled to disclose certain matters that should really be kept secret from the police. But since you people couldn't resist tracking down Gastmann and digging up the embarrassing fact that Schmied was in Lamboing, the industrialists now find themselves forced to instruct me to give the police as many details as the investigation of the Schmied case may require. The unpleasantness for us consists in having to divulge political matters of eminent importance, and the unpleasantness for you is that your authority as policemen extends to all Swiss and foreign nationals in this country *except* for the ones listed in section three."

"I don't understand a word of what you're saying," Lutz said.

"You've never understood a thing about politics, my dear Lucius," von Schwendi replied. "The third section contains the names of members of a foreign embassy. That embassy does not want to be mentioned in association with a certain class of industrialists."

Now Lutz understood the state councillor, and there was a long silence in the police chief's room. The telephone rang, and Lutz lifted the receiver only to shout the word "Conference!" into it, after which he fell silent again. At long last he spoke:

"But as far as I know, our government is now officially negotiating a new trade agreement with this same foreign power."

"That's absolutely true, negotiations are under way," the colonel replied. "Official negotiations— why not, the diplomats want to have something to do. But there are also unofficial negotiations, and in Lamboing, the negotiations are private. Modern industry, my dear Lutz, involves negotiations in which the state may not and must not interfere."

"Of course," Lutz agreed, thoroughly intimidated.

"Of course," von Schwendi repeated. "And as we now both know, the unfortunately murdered police lieutenant Ulrich Schmied secretly attended these meetings under a false name."

The police chief sat as if stunned, and von Schwendi saw that his calculation was paying off. Lutz was now so deflated that the state councillor would be able to do with him as he wished. As is frequently the case with determined and simpleminded natures, this earnest official was so upset by the unexpected developments in the Schmied murder case that he allowed himself to be influenced and made concessions that a more objective reflection would have counseled him against. To spare himself further humiliation, he tried to make light of his predicament.

"Dear Oscar," he said, "it doesn't look all that grave to me. Of course Swiss industrialists have a right to negotiate privately with whoever is interested, even with that foreign power. I would never dispute that, nor do the police interfere in these matters. I repeat, Schmied went to Gastmann on his own initiative, and I want to officially apologize for that; it was certainly irregular for him to hide behind an assumed name and pretend to have another profession, although, being a policeman myself, I can understand why he might have felt inhibited in that company. But he wasn't the only one there. What about all those artists, my dear State Councillor?"

"Decoration. We live in a cultured society, Lutz, and we need to advertise that. The negotiations have to be kept secret, and artists are good for that. Everyone dining together, a nice roast, wine, cigars, women, conversation, the artists get bored, huddle in little groups, drink, and never notice that the capitalists and the representatives of that foreign power are sitting together. They don't want to notice, because they're not interested. Artists are only interested in art. But a policeman sitting there can find out everything. No, Lutz, there's something very dubious about this Schmied of yours."

"I'm sorry, but I can only repeat that as yet, we have no clue as to why Schmied visited Gastmann."

"If the police didn't send him, someone else did," replied von Schwendi. "There are foreign powers, dear Lucius, that are interested in what's going on in Lamboing. I'm talking about world politics."

"Schmied was not a spy."

"We have every reason to suspect that he was one. It is better for Switzerland's honor if he was a spy than if he was a police agent."

"Now he is dead," sighed the police chief, who would have given anything to be able to ask Schmied himself.

"That's not our concern," said the colonel. "I don't want to cast suspicion on anyone, but the fact is that the only conceivable party interested in keeping the negotiations in Lamboing secret is that foreign power. For us, it's a question of money; for them, it's political principle. Let's not deceive ourselves. But if Schmied's death is their doing, the police will be rather severely handicapped."

Lutz stood up and went to the window. "I still don't quite see how your client Gastmann fits into this picture," he said, speaking slowly. Von Schwendi fanned himself with the large sheet of paper and replied, "Gastmann put his house at the disposal of the industrialists and diplomats attending those meetings."

"But why Gastmann?"

"My highly respected client," growled the colonel, "was a man of the requisite caliber. As a former Argentine ambassador to China, he enjoyed the trust of the foreign power, and as former chief of the tin syndicate, he had the confidence of the industrialists. And besides, he lived in Lamboing."

"How do you mean, Oscar?"

Von Schwendi smiled. "Did you ever hear of Lamboing before Schmied was murdered?"

"No."

"That's just it," said the state councillor. "No one has ever heard of Lamboing, and we needed an obscure site for our meetings. So you may as well leave Gastmann alone. I'm sure you can understand that he doesn't relish close contact with the police, that he doesn't appreciate your sniffing and prying, your endless questions. You can do that with your common crooks and gangsters, but not with a man who refused to be inducted into the French Academy. And besides, the men you sent out there couldn't have been more clumsy if they tried. You don't shoot a dog during a Bach recital. Not that Gastmann is insulted. He's completely indifferent. If your men machine-gunned his house he wouldn't raise an eyebrow. It's just that there's no sense in bothering him any longer, since the forces behind this murder have nothing to do with our decent Swiss industrialists or with Gastmann."

The police chief paced back and forth in front of the window. "We will now have to focus our investigation on Schmied's life," he said. "As for that foreign power, we will make a report to the attorney general. To what extent he will want to take over the case I can't say yet, but he will leave most of the job to us. I will comply with your request that we spare Gastmann any unnecessary inconvenience; we certainly won't search his house. However, if I should need to speak to him, I must ask you to arrange a meeting at which you would be present. That way Gastmann and I could dispose of the necessary formalities in a relaxed and casual way. I'm not talking about a formal inquest but about a formality within the framework of the inquest, since, under certain conditions, the inquest may require that we interrogate Gastmann, meaningless though that may be; but an inquest has to be complete. We'll talk about art, that'll keep the procedure as innocuous as possible, and I won't ask any questions. If I should be forced to ask a question—for formal reasons—I would let you know that question in advance."

By now, the state councillor had also risen to his feet, and the two men stood facing each other. The state councillor tapped the police chief on the shoulder.

"So we're in agreement," he said. "You will leave Gastmann alone, my dear little Lucius, I'm holding you to that. I'll leave the list with you: it's accurate and complete. I've been busy telephoning all night, everyone's very upset. No one knows whether the foreign embassy will want to continue negotiating once they learn about the Schmied case. Millions are at stake, doctor: millions! I wish you luck with your investigation. You'll need it."

With these words von Schwendi stomped out of the room.

10

Lutz had just enough time to glance through the state councillor's list, a roster of some of the nation's most illustrious names, and lower it again with a groan— good God, he thought, how did I ever get myself involved in this—when Barlach stepped in, without knocking, as usual. The old man had come to ask for authorization to interrogate Gastmann in Lamboing, but Lutz put him off until the afternoon. "It's time to go to the funeral," he said, and stood up.

Barlach did not object, and left the room with Lutz, who was beginning to regret his foolhardy promise to leave Gastmann alone. He was also beginning to fear Barlach's opinion, which was not likely to be sympathetic. They stood on the street, both of them silent, both of them dressed in black coats with turned-up collars. It was raining, but since it was just a few steps to the car, they didn't open their umbrellas. Blatter was driving. The moment they took off, the clouds burst and the rain came down in violent cascades that were driven slantwise against the car windows. Lutz and Barlach sat motionless, each in his own corner. Now I have to tell him, thought Lutz, looking at Barlach's calm profile. The inspector put his hand on his stomach.

"Are you in pain?" Lutz asked.

"Always," Barlach replied.

Then they fell silent again, and Lutz thought, I'll tell him in the afternoon. Blatter drove slowly. The downpour was so heavy that everything around them vanished behind a white wall. Somewhere, streetcars and automobiles swam about in these monstrous falling seas. Lutz did not know where they were, the dripping windows permitted no view. It was getting darker in the car. Lutz lit a cigarette, exhaled, decided to avoid any discussion of Gastmann with the old man, and said:

"The newspapers will report the murder, there was no way to keep it secret."

"There's no need to any more," Barlach said, "now that we've found a clue."

Lutz extinguished his cigarette. "There never was any need."

Barlach said nothing, and Lutz, who would have welcomed an argument, peered through the window again. The rain had begun to subside. They had already reached the avenue leading to Schlosshalden Cemetery; the gray, rain-soaked walls were pushing into view behind steaming tree trunks. Blatter drove into the courtyard and stopped. They got out of the car, opened their umbrellas, and walked through the rows of graves. They did not have to search for long. The gravestones and crosses receded; it seemed they had entered a construction site. The earth was riddled with freshly dug graves, and each grave was covered with planks. The moisture from the wet grass penetrated their mud-caked shoes. In the middle of this cleared space, surrounded by all those still tenantless graves, at the bottom of which the rain had collected in dirty puddles, among improvised wooden crosses and mounds of earth covered with heaps of rapidly rotting flowers and wreaths, a group of people was standing around a grave. The coffin had not been lowered yet. The priest was reading from the Bible. Beside him, shivering in a ludicrous work suit that resembled a frock coat, holding up an umbrella for both the priest and himself, the gravedigger was shifting his weight from one foot to the other. Barlach and Lutz stopped next to the grave. The older man heard someone crying. It was Frau Schönler's rotund, shapeless form in the ceaseless rain, and next to her stood Tschanz, without an umbrella, in a coat with the collar turned up and the belt hanging loose, a stiff black hat on his head. Next to him a girl, pale, hatless, blond hair dripping down in long strands. It occurred to Barlach that this must be Anna. Tschanz bowed, Lutz nodded, the inspector stood motionless and impassive. He looked across at the others standing around the grave, policemen, all of them, all of them out of uniform, all wearing the same raincoats, the same stiff black hats, holding their umbrellas like sabers, a group of sentries blown in from some unearthly place to watch over the dead, unreal in their earnestness. And behind them, hastily summoned from all over town and assembled in serried ranks, the municipal band in their black and red uniforms, desperately trying to protect their yellow instruments under their coats. And so they all stood around the coffin, a wooden box without a wreath, without flowers, but nevertheless the only warm and sheltering thing in this relentlessly regular pouring and dripping without foreseeable end. The priest had stopped talking a long time ago. No one noticed. There was only the rain, nothing else existed. The priest coughed. Once. Then several times. Thereupon the bassoons, French horns, cornets, trombones, and tubas blared forth in a proud and stately wail, yellow flashes of light in the floods of rain; but then they, too, subsided, faltered, gave up. Everyone crept back under umbrellas and coats. The rain was falling more and more strongly, shoes sank into the mud, rivers flowed into the empty grave. Lutz bowed and stepped forward. He looked at the wet coffin and bowed again.

"Men," he said somewhere in the rain, almost inaudible through the veils of water, "Men, our comrade Schmied is no more."

Suddenly he was interrupted by a wild, raucous song:

> "The devil goes round,
> the devil goes round,
> he beats the people into the ground!"

Two men in black frock coats came staggering across the cemetery. Without umbrellas or overcoats, they were at the mercy of the rain. Their clothes clung to their limbs. Both wore top hats from which water streamed into their faces. They were carrying an enormous laurel wreath with a ribbon that trailed in the mud. They were huge, brutal men, butchers in evening wear, drunk to the gills, constantly on the verge of keeling over, but since they never stumbled at the same time, each of them managed to hold himself up by the laurel wreath that rose and fell between them like a ship in distress. Now they launched into a new song:

> "The miller's wife, 'er 'usband is dead,
> And she is alive, alive,
> She married the miller's apprentice instead,
> And she is alive, alive."

They ran up to the group of mourners and threw themselves into their midst, right between Frau Schönler and Tschanz. No one hindered them, everyone stood as if petrified, and already they were staggering off through the wet grass, leaning upon and clinging to each other, falling over grave mounds, knocking down crosses. Their singsong died away in the rain, and everything was covered up again.

> "Everything passes,
> everything goes!"

was the last that was heard of them. Only the wreath remained. They had dropped it onto the coffin. Written in running black letters on the muddied ribbon were the words: "To our dear Dr. Prantl."

But just as the people around the grave had recovered from their shock and were about to voice their indignation, and as the municipal band burst into another desperate wail in an effort to reclaim the solemnity of the occasion, the wind and the rain started whipping about with such rampant fury that everyone fled, leaving only the gravediggers, black scarecrows in the howling torrent, to finally lower the coffin into the grave.

11

When Barlach was back in the car with his boss, and Blatter was weaving his way through fleeing policemen and musicians, Lutz finally gave vent to his anger:

"Unbelievable, this Gastmann!"

"I don't understand," the old man said.

"Schmied frequented Gastmann's house under the name of Prantl."

"In that case we've been given a warning," Barlach replied, but asked nothing further. They were driving toward Muristalden, where Lutz lived. This is the right moment, Lutz thought. Now I'll tell the old man about Gastmann, and why he must be left alone. But again he remained silent. He got out at the Burgernziel, leaving Barlach in the car.

"Shall I drive you into the city, Inspector?" asked the policeman behind the wheel.

"No, drive me home, Blatter."

Blatter drove faster now. The storm had relaxed, and suddenly, by the Muristalden, Barlach found himself steeped in blinding light: the sun broke through the clouds, disappeared, came out again, and was caught up in a rollicking chase of mists and clouds, huge bulging mounds that came racing in from the West to pile up in front of the mountains, casting wild shadows across the city that lay spread out by the river between forests and hills like a body devoid of will and resistance. Barlach's tired hand stroked his wet coat, his narrowed eyes glittered as he avidly drank in the spectacle: the world was beautiful. Blatter stopped. Barlach thanked him and got out of the car. It was no longer raining, only the wind was left, the wet, cold wind. The old man stood waiting for Blatter to turn the heavy car around, and waved once more as the policeman drove off. Then he stepped up to the edge of the Aare river. The water was high and dirty brown. A rusty old baby carriage came swimming along, branches, a small fir tree, and then, dancing, a little paper boat. Barlach watched the river for a long time, he loved it. Then he went through the garden and into the house.

Barlach changed his shoes before entering the hall. At the door to his study, he stopped. Behind the desk sat a man who was leafing through Schmied's dossier. His right hand was toying with Barlach's Turkish knife.

"So it's you," said the old man.

"Yes, it's me," said the other.

Barlach closed the door and sat down in his armchair facing the desk. Silently he watched as the other calmly turned the pages in Schmied's folder, an almost peasant-like figure, calm and withdrawn, deep-set eyes in a bony but round face, short-cropped hair.

"So you call yourself Gastmann now," the old man finally said.

The other pulled out a pipe, stuffed it without taking his eyes off Barlach, lit it, and, tapping the folder with his index finger, replied:

"You've been well aware of that for a while. It was you who set that boy at my heels. These notes are yours."

Then he closed the folder again. Barlach glanced at the desk. There was his gun, with the butt turned toward him, all he had to do was reach out. Then he said:

"I'll never stop hunting you. Some day I'll succeed in proving your crimes."

"You'll have to hurry up, Barlach," the other replied. "You don't have much time. The doctors give you another year if you let them operate on you now."

"You're right," said the old man. "One more year. And I can't let them operate now. I have to live up to this challenge. It's my last chance."

"Your last," confirmed the other, and then they both sat silently facing each other for a long time.

"It was over forty years ago that we first met," the other began again. "I'm sure you remember. It was in some tumbledown Jewish tavern in the Bosporus. There was a shapeless yellow Swiss cheese of a moon dangling between the clouds, we could see it through the rotting rafters. You, Barlach, were a young Swiss police specialist hired by the Turks to institute some sort of reform, and I—well, I was what I still am, a globetrotter, an adventurer, avid to live this one life that I have and to learn all there is to learn about this mysterious and singular planet. We loved each other at first sight, sitting there among dirty Greeks and Jews in their caftans. But when those infernal liquors we poured down our gullets, those fermented juices of God knows what sort of dates and those flaming seas from the cornfields of Odessa, when all that started boiling up inside us, making our eyes burn like glowing embers through the Turkish night, our talk started heating up. Oh, I love to think of that hour that set us both on our courses!"

He laughed.

The old man sat and watched him in silence.

"You have one more year to live," the other continued, "and for forty years you've given me a tough chase. That is the upshot. What did we talk about, Barlach, in the rot of that bar in a suburb called Tophane, swathed in Turkish cigarette smoke? Your thesis was that human imperfection—the fact that we can never predict with certainty how others will act, and that furthermore we have no way of calculating the ways chance interferes in our plans—guarantees that most crimes will perforce be detected. To commit a crime, you said, is an act of stupidity, because you can't operate with people as if they were chessmen. Against this I contended, more for the sake of argument than out of conviction, that it's precisely this incalculable, chaotic element in human relations that makes it possible to commit crimes that *cannot* be detected, and that for this reason the majority of crimes are not only not punished, but are simply not known, because, in effect, they are perfectly hidden.

"And as we kept arguing, seduced by those infernal fires the Jew kept pouring into our glasses, and even more by our own exuberant youth, we ended up making a bet, and it happened just as the moon was sinking behind Asia Minor, a wager which we defiantly pinned to the sky, very much like the kind of horrible joke that offends against everything sacred and yet holds out such a devilish appeal, such a wicked temptation of the spirit by the spirit, that we cannot suppress it."

"You're right," the old man calmly said, "that's when we made that bet."

"You didn't think I would go through with it," laughed the other, "the way we woke up in that desolate bar the next morning, you on a rotting bench and I under a table that was still soaked with liquor."

"I didn't think," Barlach replied, "that anyone would be capable of going through with it." They were silent.

"Lead us not into temptation," the other began again. "You were always such a good boy, your probity was never in danger of being tempted, but I was tempted by your probity. I kept my bold vow to commit a crime in your presence without your being able to prove that I did it."

"Three days later," the old man said softly, immersed in his memories, "we were crossing the Mahmoud Bridge with a German merchant, and you pushed him into the water in front of my eyes."

"Yes, the poor fellow couldn't swim, and your own natatory skills were so modest that after your failed attempt to rescue him they had to drag you half drowned from the dirty waters of the Golden

Horn," the other replied, unperturbed. "The murder took place on a brilliant Turkish summer day, with a pleasant breeze blowing in from the sea, on a crowded bridge in full view of amorous couples from the European colony, Muslims, and local beggars, and yet you could not prove my guilt. You had me arrested, in vain. Interrogations, hour after hour, useless. The court believed my version, that the merchant had committed suicide."

"You were able to prove that he was on the brink of bankruptcy and had tried, unsuccessfully, to save himself by committing a fraud," the old man admitted, bitterly, paler than usual.

"I chose my victim carefully, my friend," laughed the other.

"And so you became a criminal," said the inspector. The other toyed absently with the Turkish knife.

"I can't very well deny that I am something like a criminal," he finally said in a casual manner. "I became better and better at it, and you got better and better at your criminology: but I was always one step ahead of you, and you have never been able to catch up. I kept looming up in your career like some gray apparition, I couldn't resist the temptation to commit crimes right under your nose, each one bolder, wilder, and more outrageous than the last, and time after time you were unable to prove them. You could defeat fools, but I defeated you."

His gaze was amused and alert as he continued: "So that's how we lived our lives. Yours was spent in humble subordination, in police stations and musty offices, climbing the ladder of your modest achievements one rung at a time, waging war against petty forgers and thieves, poor bastards who never learned to stand up straight, a couple of pathetic murderers at best, while I ran the whole gamut of life, from the deepest obscurity, lost in the thicket of desolate cities, to the spotlight of an illustrious position, covered with medals, doing good for the sheer hell of it, and when it so pleased me, committing evil and loving it. What an adventure! Your deepest desire was to ruin my life, and mine, to spite you by living my life as I did. Truly, that one night chained us together forever!"

The man behind Barlach's desk clapped his hands together; it was one single, cruel slap. "Now we've arrived at the end of our careers," he cried. "You've come back half defeated to your dear old Bern, a sleepy, innocuous town where no one can distinguish the living from the dead, and I've come back to Lamboing, this too on the spur of a whim: it's nice to round things off, because, you see, it's in this godforsaken village that some woman long since dead gave birth to me, without much thought and very little sense, which is why I stole away one rainy night when I was thirteen years old. So here we are again. Give it up, my friend, it's pointless. Death does not wait."

And now, with an almost imperceptible movement of his hand, he threw the knife. It grazed Barlach's cheek and plunged deep into the armchair. The old man did not move. The other laughed.

"So you think I killed Schmied?"

"It's my job to investigate this case," replied the inspector.

The other stood up and took the dossier.

"I'm taking this with me."

"One day I'll succeed in proving your crimes," Barlach said for the second time. "And this is my last chance."

"Inside this briefcase is the scanty evidence Schmied collected for you in Lamboing. Without it you're lost. You don't have any copies or photostats, I know you."

"No, I don't," the old man admitted.

"How about using the gun to stop me?" the other asked with a smile.

"You took out the cartridges," Barlach replied, stone faced.

"That's right," said the other, patting him on the shoulder. Then he walked past the old man, the door opened and closed, a second door opened and closed outside. Barlach was still sitting in his armchair, leaning his cheek against the cold blade of the knife. But suddenly he seized the gun and opened it. It was loaded. He jumped up, ran into the vestibule, tore open the front door, gun in hand:

The street was empty.

Then came the pain, the overwhelming, monstrous, stabbing pain, a sun rising inside him, it threw him onto the couch, convulsed him, scalded and shook him with feverish heat. The old man crawled on his hands and knees like an animal, threw himself on the ground, dragged himself across the rug, and finally lay still somewhere in his room between the chairs, covered with cold sweat. "What is man?" he moaned softly. "What is man?"

12

But he recovered. After the attack, he felt an unusual sensation: complete freedom from pain. He heated some wine and drank it in small, careful sips. That was all he ate or drank. He didn't refrain, however, from taking his customary walk though the city and across the Bundesterrasse. He was still half unconscious, but the air was so pure, as if washed by the storm, that he felt himself reviving with each step.

When Lutz saw Barlach come into his office, he noticed nothing; perhaps he was too preoccupied with his own bad conscience. He decided to tell Barlach about his talk with von Schwendi right away, instead of waiting till the end of the day. For this purpose, he assumed a cold impersonal stance, puffing out his chest like the general in Traffelet's picture above him, and briefed the old man in a clipped and curt telegram style. But to his boundless surprise, the inspector raised no objection. He was in complete agreement: pending instructions from the federal government, the investigation should be limited to an examination of Schmied's life. Lutz was so surprised that he gave up his pose and became chatty and affable.

"Naturally I've found out some things about Gastmann," he said, "and I know enough about him to be certain that he couldn't possibly be the killer."

"Of course," the old man said.

Lutz, who had received some new data from Biel during his lunch hour, put on an air of assurance.

"Born in Pockau, Saxony, son of a leather merchant. Starts out as an Argentinian—must have emigrated as a young man, serves as Argentine ambassador to China. After that he's French, usually away on some long trip abroad. He was awarded the Cross of the Foreign Legion and is known as a scientist, published several works on questions of biology. As for his character: the man was elected to the French Academy and declined to accept the honor. I find that impressive."

"Interesting trait," Barlach said.

"We're still investigating his two servants. They have French passports, but it seems they're from the Emmental. That was a nasty joke he had them play on us at the funeral."

"That appears to be Gastmann's sense of humor," the old man said.

"He's probably upset about the death of his dog. But we have even greater cause to be upset. This whole Schmied case is putting us in a very wrong light. We can count ourselves lucky that I'm on friendly terms with von Schwendi. Gastmann is a man of international cachet, and he enjoys the full confidence of Swiss industrialists."

"Then he must be all right," Barlach said.

"His character is above all suspicion."

"Definitely," the old man nodded.

"Unfortunately we can no longer say the same about Schmied." With these words, Lutz concluded the conversation. He picked up the receiver and asked the operator to connect him with the House of Parliament.

But as Lutz sat waiting with the receiver against his ear, the inspector, who had already turned to leave, stopped and said:

"I have to ask you for a week's sick leave, Dr. Lutz."

"That's quite all right," Lutz said, covering the mouthpiece with his palm, since the call was coming through. "You needn't come in on Monday."

Tschanz was waiting in Barlach's office. He stood up when the old man came in. He had a calm demeanor, but the inspector sensed that the policeman was nervous.

"Let's drive out to Gastmann's house," Tschanz said, "it's high time we did that."

"To the writer," the old man replied, and put on his coat.

"Detours, nothing but detours," Tschanz said angrily as he followed Barlach down the stairs. The inspector stopped in the front door:

"There's Schmied's blue Mercedes."

Tschanz said he had bought it, on an installment plan. "Someone has to own it," he said, and got in. Barlach sat down next to him, and Tschanz drove across the Bahnhofplatz toward Bethlehem hospital. Barlach grumbled:

"You're driving via Ins again."

"I love this route."

Barlach rested his eyes on the fields that had been washed clean by the rain. Everything was steeped in

76

a calm, bright light. The sun in the sky was mild and warm and was already sinking toward evening. Both men were silent. Only once, between Kerzers and Muntschemier, did Tschanz speak.

"Frau Schönler told me you took a folder from Schmied's room."

"Nothing official, Tschanz, just personal things."

Tschanz made no comment and asked no more questions. But Barlach had to tap his finger against the speedometer, which was showing eighty miles an hour.

"Not so fast, Tschanz, not so fast. Not that I'm scared, but my stomach can't take it. I'm an old man."

13

The writer received them in his study. It was an old, low-ceilinged room, and as the two men stepped in they were forced to stoop as if under a yoke. Outside, the little white dog with the black head was still barking, and somewhere in the house a child was crying. The writer sat in front by the gothic window, dressed in overalls and a brown leather jacket. He swiveled in his chair to face the visitors. Without rising from his desk, which was covered with papers, and after a perfunctory greeting, he demanded to know what the police wanted of him. "He's impolite," Barlach thought, "and he doesn't like policemen. Writers have never liked policemen." The old man decided to be careful. Tschanz, too, was unpleasantly affected. "He's observing us," they both thought. "If we don't watch out, we'll end up in a book." With a gesture of his hand, the writer invited them to sit down. But the moment they sank into the soft armchairs, they noted with surprise that they were seated in the light of the small window, and that the writer in his low green room filled with books was cunningly hidden from their view by the glare that fell into their eyes.

"We're looking into the case of police officer Schmied," the old man began, "who was murdered above Twann."

"I know. The case of Doctor Prantl, who was spying on Gastmann," replied the dark mass between the window and themselves. "Gastmann told me about it." For a brief moment the writer's face was revealed as he lit a cigarette. A grin twisted his features. "You want my alibi?" Then the match went out.

"No," Barlach said.

"You don't think I could have committed the murder?" asked the writer, noticeably disappointed.

"No," Barlach replied dryly, "not you."

The writer moaned. "There we are again. Writers are sadly underestimated in Switzerland!"

The old man laughed. "If you really want to know: we already have your alibi, naturally. At twelve thirty on the night of the murder you met the bailiff and walked home together with him. The bailiff said you were in high spirits."

"I know. The policeman of Twann questioned the bailiff twice about me. And everyone who lives here. Even my mother-in-law. So you did suspect me after all," the writer noted with pride. "That's literary success of a sort!" And Barlach thought: so that's the famous vanity of writers, this craving to be taken seriously. All three men fell silent, and Tschanz tried hard to make out the writer's features. It was impossible to see him in this light.

"So what else do you want?" the writer finally hissed.

"Do you see Gastmann often?"

"What is this—an interrogation?" asked the dark mass, pushing itself more squarely in front of the window. "I don't have time for that right now."

"Come on, don't be so mean," said the inspector.

"All we want is to talk a little." The writer let out a grunt, Barlach began again. "Do you see Gastmann often?"

"Now and then."

"Why?"

The old man expected another angry reply; but the writer just laughed, blew a big cloud of smoke in both their faces, and replied:

"He's an interesting character, this Gastmann, Inspector, he's the type who attracts writers like flies. And he's a wonderful cook, just amazing, let me tell you!"

And tell them he did. He told of Gastmann's culinary artistry, describing one dish after the other. For five minutes the policemen paid polite attention, and then for another five minutes; but when, after fifteen minutes, the writer was still singing the praises of Gastmann's cooking, Tschanz stood up and said he was sorry, but he and his colleague had not come to discuss food. Barlach however, whose spirits had thoroughly revived, contradicted him. "Not true," he said, "I'm extremely interested in this subject," and proceeded to rhapsodize about the culinary magic of the Turks, the Romanians, the Bulgarians, the Yugoslavs, the Czechs, until the two men were tossing exotic recipes back and forth with the tireless enthusiasm of boys playing catch. Tschanz was sweating and cursing under his breath. The delights of the palate were quite evidently infinite and inexhaustible. But finally, after forty-five minutes, the two men stopped, exhausted, as if they had eaten long and heartily and had reached the end of their appetite. The writer lit himself a cigar. The room was silent. The child next door started crying again. The dog was barking downstairs. Then Tschanz suddenly spoke.

"Did Gastmann kill Schmied?"

The question was primitive, the old man shook his head, and the dark mass in front of them said, "You don't beat around the bush, do you?"

"I would appreciate an answer," Tschanz said firmly, leaning forward. But the writer's face remained hidden in darkness.

Barlach wondered how the man would react.

The writer remained calm.

"When was the policeman killed?" he asked.

"Before midnight," Tschanz replied.

"I don't know whether the rules of logic apply for the police," the writer said. "I rather doubt it. But since the police so cleverly found out that I met the bailiff at twelve thirty on the road to Tschernelz, it would seem that I must have taken leave of Gastmann no more than ten minutes earlier, in which case Gastmann is not very likely to have been the killer."

Tschanz wanted to know whether any other guests were present at Gastmann's at that time.

The writer answered in the negative.

"Did Schmied leave with the others?"

"Doctor Prantl was in the habit of being the penultimate guest to leave the party," the writer replied with a touch of sarcasm.

"And the last to leave?"

"That was me."

Tschanz wouldn't let go. "Were both servants present?"

"I don't know."

"How about a straight answer."

"You got a straight answer. I never pay attention to this type of servant."

With a desperation and lack of restraint that made the inspector feel acutely uncomfortable, Tschanz demanded to know whether the writer considered Gastmann a good or a bad man. "If we don't end up in his next novel," Barlach thought, "it'll be a miracle."

The writer blew such a thick cloud of smoke in Tschanz's face that the officer began to cough. Then silence descended on the room again. Even the child next door was quiet.

"Gastmann is a bad man," the writer finally said.

"And yet you keep visiting him, and for no other reason than that he's a good cook?" Tschanz asked indignantly after recovering from another coughing spell.

"For no other reason."

"I don't understand that."

The writer laughed. "I'm kind of a policeman myself," he said. "Except I have no state power, no body of laws, and no prisons to back me up. But my job is a lot like yours: I keep an eye on people."

Bewildered, Tschanz stopped asking questions, and Barlach said, "I understand." After a while, he added:

"I'm afraid that in his exaggerated zeal my subordinate Tschanz has forced us into an impasse from which I won't escape without losing a few hairs. But youthful impetuousness has its good points. Now that an unbridled ox has trampled a path for us" (Tschanz grew red with anger when the inspector said this), "let's stay with the questions and answers that have already fallen and make the best of them—take the bull by the horns, if you will. What is your opinion of this whole affair, sir? Is Gastmann capable of committing murder?"

It had become darker in the room, but it didn't occur to the writer to turn on the light. Instead he sat down in the windowsill, leaving the two policemen crouching in their armchairs like prisoners in a cave.

"I believe Gastmann is capable of every imaginable crime." The voice from the window was brutal, with a hint of sly malice in it. "But I am convinced that he is not the man who murdered Schmied."

"You know Gastmann well," Barlach said.

"I'm starting to get a picture of him," the writer said.

"*Your* picture of him," the old man coolly corrected the massive silhouette in the window sill.

"What fascinates me about him is not so much his cooking—though I must say there's hardly anything else that thrills me these days—but that here is a man who is actually—not just possibly—a nihilist," said the writer. "A slogan in the flesh. It takes your breath away."

"Listening to a writer takes your breath away too," the inspector remarked dryly.

"Maybe Gastmann has done more good than the three of us sitting here in this crooked little room," the writer continued. "When I say he's bad, it's because good and evil are, for him, just a matter of whim, and he would go to any length in either direction simply because the mood strikes him. He would never do anything evil just for the sake of gain, the way others commit crimes, for money, women, or power. But he would do it for no reason at all—maybe. Because for him, two things are always possible, good and evil, and it's chance that decides which it will be."

"You're deducing this as if it were mathematics," the old man retorted.

"It is mathematics," the writer replied. "You could construct his counterpart in evil the way you can construct a geometric figure as the mirror image of another one, and I'm sure that there is such a man— somewhere. Maybe you'll meet him too. If you meet the one, you'll meet the other."

"Sounds like a program," the old man said.

"Well, it is a program, and why not," said the writer. "My idea of Gastmann's mirror image is a man who would be a criminal because the idea of evil represents his ethics, his philosophy, to which he would be as fanatically committed as a saint might be devoted to the good."

The inspector suggested they get back to Gastmann, who was closer to his immediate interests.

"As you wish," said the writer. "Back to Gastmann, Inspector. Back to this one pole of evil. For him evil is not the expression of a philosophy or a biological drive, it is his freedom: the freedom of nothingness."

"Some freedom. I wouldn't give a cent for it," the old man replied.

"Nor should you give a cent for it," returned the other. "But one could spend a lifetime studying this man and this freedom of his."

"A lifetime," said the old man.

The writer was silent. He seemed unwilling to say anything further.

"I'm dealing with a real Gastmann," the old man finally said. "With a man who lives near Lamlingen on the Tessenberg plain and gives parties that cost a police lieutenant his life. I have to know whether the picture you have drawn for me is a picture of Gastmann or a product of your imagination."

"Our imagination," the writer said.

The inspector said nothing.

"I don't know," the writer said. He rose from his seat and stepped up to his visitors. Evidently he expected them to leave. He shook Barlach's hand, and not Tschanz's. "That's something I've never concerned myself with," he said. "I leave that to the police."

14

The two policemen walked back to their car, followed by the little white dog, which barked at them furiously, and Tschanz sat down at the wheel.

"I don't like this writer," he said. Bärlach arranged his coat before he got in. The little dog had climbed onto a low stone wall and continued barking.

"Now to Gastmann's place," Tschanz said, and started the motor. The old man shook his head.

"To Bern."

They drove downhill in the direction of Ligerz, into a land that opened out far below, at a tremendous depth. All around them, the elements lay spread out far and wide: stone, earth, and water. They were driving in the shade, but the sun, which had sunk behind the Tessenberg, was still shining on the lake, the island, the hills, the foothills of the mountains, the glaciers on the horizon, and the immense towering heaps of cloud floating along in the blue oceans of the sky. The old man gazed steadily at the ceaselessly shifting, already wintry weather. It's always the same, he thought, no matter how much it changes it's always the same. But as the road suddenly swerved and the lake lay vertically beneath them like a bulging shield, Tschanz stopped the car.

"I have to talk to you, Inspector," he said in an agitated tone.

"What do you want?" Barlach asked, looking down at the huge drop by the side of the road.

"We have to see Gastmann, it's logical, it's the only lead we've got. And above all, we have to question his servants."

Barlach leaned back and sat there, gray and well groomed, scrutinizing the young man by his side through cold, narrowed eyes.

"My God, Tschanz, we can't always do the logical thing. Lutz doesn't want us to visit Gastmann. That's understandable, since he had to hand over the case to the attorney general. Let's wait for the government's ruling. It's a touchy business, we're dealing with foreigners." Barlach's casual manner drove Tschanz into a rage.

"That's nonsense!" he shouted. "Lutz is sabotaging the investigation for political reasons. Von Schwendi is his friend and Gastmann's lawyer, don't you see what's going on?"

Not a muscle moved in Barlach's face. "It's good that we're alone, Tschanz. Lutz may have acted prematurely, but his reasons were sound. The mystery lies with Schmied and not with Gastmann."

"It's our job to look for the truth!" Tschanz shouted the words into the mountainous clouds drifting overhead. "The truth and nothing but the truth! The truth about Schmied's murderer!"

"You're right," Barlach repeated, coldly and unemotionally. "The truth about Schmied's murderer."

The young policeman placed his hand on the old

man's left shoulder and looked into his impenetrable face.

"And that's why we have to use every means at our disposal. And use them against Gastmann. If this is going to be a real investigation, it can't have any holes in it. You say we can't always do the logical thing. But in this case we *have* to. We can't skip Gastmann."

"Gastmann is not the killer," Barlach said dryly.

"It's possible that Gastmann ordered the killing. We have to interrogate the servants!" Tschanz retorted.

"I don't see the slightest reason why Gastmann should have wanted Schmied dead," the old man said. "We must look for the criminal where the crime would make sense, and that, I'm afraid, is the attorney general's business and not ours," he continued.

"The writer also thinks Gastmann did it," Tschanz exclaimed.

"You think so too?" Barlach asked, with a glowering look.

"Me too, Inspector."

"Then you're the only one," Barlach noted. "The writer just considers him capable of any crime under the sun, there's a difference. The writer didn't say a thing about Gastmann's actions, only about his potential."

Now Tschanz lost his patience. He gripped the old man's shoulders.

"For years I've stood in the shadow, Inspector," he gasped. "I've always been left out, ignored, treated like dirt, like some kind of glorified mailman!"

"I won't deny it, Tschanz," Barlach said, still staring fixedly into the young man's desperate eyes. "For years you stood in the shadow of the man who has now been murdered."

"Just because he went to better schools! Just because he knew Latin."

"You're not being fair to him," Barlach replied. "Schmied was the best criminologist I have ever known."

"And now," Tschanz shouted, "now that I finally have an opportunity, I'm expected to let it go down the drain, my one chance to get a promotion—all because of some stupid diplomatic maneuver! Only you can change this, Inspector, talk to Lutz, only you can get him to let me go to Gastmann."

"No, Tschanz," Barlach said, "I can't do that." His subordinate shook him, as if trying to shake sense into a naughty boy, and then he screamed:

"Talk to Lutz, talk to him!"

But the old man would not be swayed. "I can't, Tschanz," he said. "I'm not up for this sort of thing any more. I'm old and sick. I need some rest. You'll have to help yourself."

"Very well," Tschanz said, abruptly taking his hands off Barlach and putting them on the wheel again. He was quivering and deathly pale. "Then don't. You can't help me."

They drove on downhill toward Ligerz.

"You spent your vacation in Grindelwald, didn't you?" the old man asked. "Pension Eiger?"

"Yes, sir."

"Quiet and not too expensive?"

"Just as you say, sir."

"Very well, Tschanz, I'll be driving there tomorrow morning for a rest. I need the altitude. I have a week's sick leave."

Tschanz did not answer immediately. Only after they had turned onto the Neuenburg–Biel highway, he said, and his voice sounded normal again:

"Altitude isn't always the best thing, Inspector."

15

That same evening Barlach went to the Bärenplatz to see his internist, Dr. Samuel Hungertobel. The streetlights were already lit, night was closing in, the darkness deepening by the minute. Barlach looked down on the old square from the doctor's window, watched the surging flood of people while Hungertobel packed up his instruments. Barlach and Hungertobel's acquaintance went back to their boyhood; they had gone to school together.

"Your heart's in good shape," Hungertobel said. "Thank God."

"Have you kept notes on my case?" Barlach asked him.

"A whole briefcase full," the doctor replied, pointing to a stack of papers on his desk. "That's all about your illness."

"You haven't told anyone about my illness, have you, Hungertobel?" Barlach asked.

"But Hans?!" said the other old man, "that's confidential, you know that!"

Down on the square, a Mercedes appeared. Its bright blue color lit up as it rolled under a light. Then it stopped among several parked cars. Barlach narrowed his eyes to see more clearly. Tschanz stepped out, followed by a young woman with a white raincoat and long blond flowing hair.

"Did anyone ever break in here, Samuel?" the inspector asked.

"Why do you ask?"

"Just wondering."

"There was a day when my desk was messed up," Hungertobel said. "And your case history was lying on top of the desk. No money had been taken, even though there was plenty inside the desk."

"And why didn't you report it?"

The doctor scratched his head. "As I said, no money had been taken. Actually I wanted to report it anyway. But then I forgot about it."

"I see," Barlach said. "You forgot. I guess burglars can count on you." And he thought: "So that's how Gastmann knows." He looked down at the square again. Tschanz was entering the Italian restaurant with the young woman. "On the day of his funeral," Barlach thought, and turned away from the window. He looked at Hungertobel, who was sitting at his desk, writing.

"So how am I doing?"

"Are you having any pains?"

The old man told him about his attack.

"That's bad news, Hans," Hungertobel said. "We'll have to operate within the next three days. There's no other way."

"I feel better than ever."

"In four days you'll have another attack, Hans," said the doctor, "and that one you won't survive."

"So I've got two days left. Two days. And on the

92

morning of the third day, you'll perform the operation. Tuesday morning."

"Tuesday morning," Hungertobel said.

"And after that I'll have another year to live, right, Samuel?" Barlach said, fixing an impenetrable gaze on his old friend. Hungertobel jumped up and paced through the room.

"Where did you get this nonsense!"

"From the person who read my case history."

"Are you the burglar?" the doctor exclaimed in great agitation.

Barlach shook his head. "No, it wasn't me. But it's a fact nonetheless, Samuel: just one more year."

"Just one more year," Hungertobel replied, sat down on a chair that stood against the wall of his office, and looked helplessly at Barlach, who was standing in the middle of the room, looking cold and remote in his isolation, stolid and humble, and with such a forlorn expression on his face that the doctor lowered his eyes.

16

Barlach woke with a start at two o'clock in the morning. At first he attributed his abrupt awakening to the effects of Hungertobel's unaccustomed prescription: he had gone to bed early and, for the first time, taken a sleeping pill. But then it seemed to him that he had been roused by some kind of noise. He was preternaturally alert and clearheaded, as often happens when we wake with a start; nevertheless it took a few moments—each one of which seemed an eternity—before he found his bearings. He was not in the room where he usually slept, but in the library; for he had anticipated a difficult night and had intended to read; but he must have suddenly fallen into a deep sleep. He passed his hands over his body. He was still dressed, and had merely covered himself with a woolen blanket. He listened. Something fell to the floor; it was the book he had been reading. The darkness in the windowless room was profound, but not complete; a weak light came in through the open door of the bedroom, the flickering glow of the stormy night. He heard the wind howling from afar. Gradually he made out the forms of a bookcase and a chair, and the edge of the table, and on top of it his revolver. Then he suddenly felt a draft, a window banged in the bedroom, and the door closed with a violent bang. Immediately afterward the old man heard a slight clicking noise in the hallway.

He understood. Someone had opened the front door and had entered the hall without considering the possibility of a draft. Barlach stood up and turned on the floor lamp.

He took the revolver and released the safety catch. At that moment the intruder turned on the light in the hallway. Barlach, who could see the shining lamp through the half open door, was surprised, for he could see no meaning in this action. By the time he understood, it was too late. He saw the silhouette of an arm and a hand reaching into the lamp; then the flare of a blue light, and darkness: the stranger had torn the lamp out of the ceiling and blown the fuse. Barlach stood in complete darkness. The intruder had taken up the challenge and set the conditions: Barlach would have to fight in the dark. The old man gripped his weapon and cautiously opened the door to the bedroom. He entered the room. A vague light fell through the windows, hardly discernible at first, but stronger as the eyes became accustomed to it. Barlach leaned against the wall between the bed and the window facing the river; the other window, facing the neighbor's house, was on his right. Thus he stood in impenetrable shadow. The disadvantage of his position was that he could not retreat, but he hoped his invisibility would make up for that. The door to the library stood in the dim light of the windows. He would see the outline of the stranger's body if he came in. Now the narrow beam of a flashlight flared in the library, glided searchingly along the books, across the floor, the armchair, and finally reached the desk, revealing the snake-knife. Again Barlach saw the hand through the open door. It was sheathed in a brown leather glove. It groped along the table and grasped the handle of the snake-knife. Barlach raised the gun, aimed. The flashlight went out. Foiled, the old man lowered his weapon and waited. Looking out the window from where he stood, he sensed the black volumes of ceaselessly roiling water, the towering structures of the city on the other side of the river, the cathedral stabbing the sky like an arrow, and above it the drifting clouds. He stood immobile, waiting for the enemy who had come to kill him. His eyes bored through the vague opening of the door. He waited. Everything was quiet, lifeless. Then the clock struck in the hallway: three. He listened. Faintly he heard the distant ticking of the clock. Somewhere a car honked, then it drove by. People leaving a bar. Once he thought he heard breathing, but he must have been mistaken. And so he stood there, and somewhere in his house was the other man, and engulfing them both, the black cloak of night, with the snake concealed beneath it, the dagger in search of his heart. The old man scarcely breathed. He stood clutching his gun, scarcely aware of the cold sweat running down his neck. He thought of nothing—not of Gastmann, not of Lutz, nor of the sickness gnawing at his body hour after hour and about to destroy the life he was now defending for no other reason than that he desperately wanted to live, and only to live. His whole being was reduced

to a single eye searching the night, a single ear test-
ing the minutest sound, a single hand firmly locked
around the cool metal of the gun. When the murderer's presence betrayed itself to him, it wasn't as he
had expected; he sensed a vague coldness touching
his cheek, a slight change in the air. For a long time
he could not explain it to himself, until he guessed
that the door leading from the bedroom to the dining
room had opened. The stranger had outwitted the
old man again, he had penetrated the bedroom by
a roundabout route, invisible, inaudible, inexorable,
with the snake-knife in his hand. Barlach knew now
that he had to be the first to act. Old and mortally sick
as he was, he would have to begin the battle, the fight
for a life that might last one more year, provided that
Hungertobel applied his knife wisely and accurately.
Barlach aimed his revolver at the window facing the
Aare River. Then he fired, and again, three times in
rapid succession through the splintering glass out into
the river, and lowered himself to the floor. He heard
a hissing sound above him. It was the knife that now
stuck in the wall, quivering. But already the old man
had achieved what he wanted: light appeared in the
other window, it came from the house next door, the
neighbors were leaning out of their opened windows;
bewildered and terrified, they were staring into the
night. Barlach rose to his feet. The neighbors' lights
lit up the bedroom. A shadowy form slipped away from
the dining room door. Then the front door slammed
shut, and after that, pulled by the draft, the door to

the library slammed, and following that the dining room door, one crash after the other, and finally the window knocked against its frame. The people next door were still staring into the night. The old man by the wall did not move. He stood there, immobile, still holding the weapon, as if he had lost all consciousness of time. The neighbors withdrew, and turned off their lights. Barlach stood by the wall, steeped in darkness again, at one with it, alone in the house.

17

Half an hour passed before he went to the hallway and looked for his flashlight. He called up Tschanz and asked him to come. Then he replaced the blown fuse, and the lights went on again. Barlach sat down in his armchair and listened into the night. A car drove up in the front of the house, braked sharply. Again the front door opened, again he heard a step. Tschanz came into the room.

"Someone tried to kill me," the inspector said. Tschanz was pale. He was hatless, his hair was disheveled, his pajama pants showed at the bottom of his winter coat. Together they went into the bedroom. With an effort, Tschanz pulled the knife out of the wall. It was deeply embedded in the wood.

"With this?"

"With that, Tschanz."

The young policeman examined the shattered windowpane.

"You shot through the window, Inspector?" he asked, surprised.

Barlach told him everything. "That was the best thing you could do," Tschanz murmured.

They went into the hallway, and Tschanz picked up the lamp from the floor.

"Clever," he said, not without admiration, and put it aside. Then they went back to the library. The old man stretched out on the couch, covered himself with the blanket, and lay there, helpless, feeling suddenly terribly old, almost shriveled. Tschanz was still holding the snake knife in his hand.

"Didn't you get a glimpse of him?" he asked.

"No. He was careful and withdrew quickly. All I saw for a moment was a brown leather glove."

"That's not much."

"It's nothing. But even though I didn't see him, even though I could hardly hear him breathe, I know who it was. I know it; I know it."

The old man said all this almost inaudibly. Tschanz weighed the knife in his hand, looking down at the gray, prostrate figure before him, this tired old man, these hands that lay next to the frail old body like withered flowers next to a corpse. Then he saw Barlach's gaze. It was focused on him, calm, clear, and inscrutable. Tschanz laid the knife on the desk.

"You must go to Grindelwald this morning, you're sick. Or would you rather not go? It might not be the right thing, the altitude. It's really winter up there."

"No, no, I'm going."

"Then you should get some sleep. Do you want me to stay here and keep watch?"

"No, Tschanz, you can go," the inspector said.

"Good night," Tschanz said and slowly walked out. The old man said nothing; he seemed to have fallen asleep. Tschanz opened the front door, stepped out, closed the door. Slowly he walked the few steps to the street, closed the garden door, which had stood open.

Then he turned toward the house again. It was still pitch dark. All things seemed lost in the night, even the houses next door. A single street light burned far above, a lost star in the gloom of a night filled with sorrow, filled with the dark steady surge of the river. Tschanz stood there, and suddenly he cursed softly under his breath. He kicked open the garden gate and strode resolutely up the path to the front door, the same way he had come. He grasped the door handle and pushed it down. But now the door was locked.

Barlach got up at six without having slept. It was Sunday. The old man washed, changed his clothes. Then he called for a taxi, intending to eat in the dining car. He put on his warm winter coat and left the house, stepping out into the cold winter morning, but without a valise. The sky was clear. A drunken student staggered by, stinking of beer, and greeted him. "Poor Blaser," Barlach thought. "He just failed his exam for the second time. No wonder he's drinking." The taxi drove up, stopped. It was one of those large American cars. The driver had turned up his collar; Barlach could hardly see his eyes. The driver opened the door for him.

"To the station," Barlach said, getting in. The car started.

"Well," said a voice next to him, "how are you? Did you sleep well?"

Barlach turned his head. In the other corner sat Gastmann. He was wearing a gray raincoat and his arms were folded. He was wearing brown leather gloves. The way he sat there, he looked like a mocking old peasant. The driver in front turned his head and looked back at Barlach, grinning. He was one of the servants. Barlach realized he had stepped into a trap.

"What do you want from me now?" he asked.

"You're still after me. You talked to that writer," said the one in the corner, and his voice sounded threatening.

"It's my job."

The other kept his eyes on him. "There isn't a single one who took up my case, Barlach, who's still alive."

The man in front drove up the Aargauerstalden at a furious speed.

"I'm still alive. And I've always been on your case," the inspector said calmly.

They were both silent.

Still racing, the driver headed for Viktoriaplatz. An old man limping across the street got out of the way in the nick of time.

"Why don't you watch what you're doing!" Barlach said angrily.

"Drive faster," Gastmann said with a cutting voice. His eyes looked mocking as he scrutinized the old man. "I love the speed of machines."

The inspector shuddered. He did not like being enclosed in an airless space. They flew across the bridge, passing a streetcar, over the silver ribbon of water far below them into the welcoming streets of the city, which were still vacant and deserted, under a glassy sky.

"I would advise you to give up," Barlach said, stuffing his pipe. "You've lost the game, it's time to concede."

The old man looked at the dark arcades gliding past them, and he noticed the shadowy figures of two policemen in front of Lang's book store.

"Geissbühler and Zumsteg," he thought, and then: "I really should pay for that Fontane novel."

"Our game," he finally replied, "—we can't give it up. You became guilty on that night in Turkey because you proposed a bet, Gastmann, and I became guilty because I accepted it."

They drove past the House of Parliament.

"You still think I killed Schmied?" Gastmann asked.

"I didn't believe that for a moment," the old man replied. He watched indifferently as the other man lit his pipe, and continued:

"I haven't succeeded in proving your guilt of the crimes you've committed. So this time I'll prove you guilty of something you didn't do."

Gastmann scrutinized the inspector's face.

"I never thought of this possibility," he said. "I'll have to be careful."

The inspector said nothing.

"You may be more dangerous than I realized, old man," Gastmann said pensively from his corner.

The car stopped. They had reached the train station.

"This is the last time I'll be talking to you, Barlach," Gastmann said. "The next time I'll kill you. Assuming you survive your operation."

"You're wrong," Barlach said, looking old as he stood shivering on the square in the early morning light. "You won't kill me. I am the only one who knows you, so I'm the only one who can judge you. I have judged you, Gastmann, I have sentenced you to death. You will not survive this day. The executioner I have chosen will come to you today. He will kill you, because, by God, this is something that simply has to be done."

Gastmann flinched and stared at the old man in astonishment. But Barlach walked into the station with his hands buried in his coat pockets. Without turning around, he walked into the dark building, which was gradually filling up with people.

"You fool!" Gastmann suddenly shouted after the inspector, so loudly that several passersby turned around. "Fool!" But Barlach was no longer visible.

18

The gradually, steadily rising day was clear and powerful. The sun, a perfect ball, cast hard and long shadows, which became shorter the higher it rolled. The city lay there, a white shell, sucking up the light, swallowing it into her narrow streets in order to spew it out after nightfall as thousands of lights, a monster perpetually busy with spawning and poisoning and burying an ever-growing quantity of new human beings. The radiance of the morning grew by the minute, a shining shield above the diminishing echoes of the church bells. Tschanz waited for an hour, looking pale in the light that was reflected from the walls. Restlessly he walked to and fro beneath the arcades in front of the cathedral, looking up at the gargoyles from time to time, demons that stared at the sunlit pavement with savage, contorted expressions. Finally the portals opened, releasing a vast stream of people who had come to hear Luthi, the famous preacher, in person, but Tschanz immediately saw her white raincoat. Anna walked up to him. She said she was glad to see him and gave him her hand. They walked up the Kesslergasse, surrounded by a swarm of churchgoers, old and young: here a professor, there a baker's wife in her Sunday finery, two students with a girl, several dozen officials, teachers, all of them clean, all of them washed, all of them hungry, all of them looking forward to a sumptuous Sunday meal. They reached the Kasinoplatz, crossed it, and went down into the Marzili. They stopped on the bridge.

"Fräulein Anna," Tschanz said, "today I'm going to catch Ulrich's murderer."

"Do you know who he is?" she asked, surprised.

He looked at her. She stood before him, pale and slim. "I believe I do," he said. "Once I've caught him, will you be . . ." He hesitated. "Will you be for me what you were for your deceased fiancé?"

Anna did not answer immediately. She pulled her coat more tightly around her as if she were cold. A slight breeze disturbed her blond hair. Then she said:

"We've agreed on that."

They shook hands, and Anna walked on to the other shore. He looked after her. Her white coat gleamed among the birch trees, disappeared among other pedestrians, reemerged, and finally vanished. Then he went to the train station, where he had left his car. He drove to Ligerz. It was almost noon when he got there, for he drove slowly, stopping occasionally to walk in the fields and smoke before returning to the car and driving on. In Ligerz he parked in front of the station. Then he climbed the steps leading up to the church. He was calm now. The lake was deep blue, the vines had lost their leaves, and the earth between them was brown and loose. But Tschanz saw none of these things. He climbed at a steady and regular pace, without turning back and without pausing. The path led steeply uphill, framed by white walls, past vineyard after vineyard. Tschanz kept climbing, calmly, slowly, steadily, his right hand in the pocket of his coat. From time to time lizards crossed his path. Buzzards rose into the sky, the land trembled under the blazing sun as if it were summer. He climbed on and on, relentlessly, unremittingly. Later he left the vineyards and slipped into the forest. It was cooler there. The Jura cliffs shone stark and white between the tree trunks. He climbed higher and higher, always at the same pace, until he reached the fields. This was farming and pasture land; the path rose more gently. He walked past a cemetery, a rectangle bordered by a gray wall, with a wide-open gate. Black-clad women walked on the paths, a bent old man stood watching the stranger as he marched past with his right hand in his coat pocket.

He reached Prèles, walked past the Bear Inn and directed his steps toward Lamboing. The air over the high plateau was motionless and clear. All things, even those in the far distance, stood out with extreme clarity. Only the ridge of the Chasseral was covered with snow, everything else was a brilliant light brown interspersed here and there with white walls and red roofs and black bands of farmland. Steadily, Tschanz walked on; the sun was shining on his back, casting his shadow ahead of him. The road dipped, he was approaching the sawmill, now the sun was at his side. He marched without thinking, without seeing, impelled by *one* purpose, possessed by *one* passion. A dog barked somewhere, came up to him, sniffed at his feet, and ran away. Tschanz walked on, always on the right-hand side of the street, always at the same pace, toward the house that was now rising up from the brown landscape, framed by bare poplars. Tschanz left the road and walked through the fields. His shoes sank into the warm earth of an unploughed field; he walked on. Then he reached the gate. It was open; Tschanz went through it. In the courtyard stood an American car. Tschanz payed it no attention. He went to the front door. It, too, was open. Tschanz stepped into an entrance hall, opened a second door, and walked into a hall that comprised the whole ground floor. Tschanz stopped. Glaring light fell through the windows facing him. In front of him, not five paces away, stood Gastmann. Next to him his gigantic servants, immobile and menacing, two butchers. All three were wearing coats. Towering heaps of valises stood by their sides. They were about to leave.

Tschanz stood still.

"So it's you," Gastmann said, looking with slight surprise at the calm, pale face of the policeman and at the open door behind him.

Then he started to laugh. "So that's what the old man meant! Not bad, not bad at all!"

Gastmann's eyes were wide open, and Tschanz saw them light up with a flash of ghostly mirth.

Calmly, without saying a word, almost slowly, one of the butchers pulled a pistol out of his pocket and fired. Tschanz felt a blow against his left shoulder, pulled his right hand out of his pocket and threw himself to the side. Then he fired three shots point blank into Gastmann's laughter, which died away slowly as if in an infinite void.

19

Informed by a telephone call from Tschanz, Charnel sped over from Lamboing, Clenin rushed in from Twann, and the crime squad from Biel. Tschanz was found bleeding near the three corpses. A second shot had hit him in the left forearm. The gun battle must have been brief, but each of the three dead men had found time to fire. A gun was found on each of them. One of the servants was still holding his weapon in a tight grip. Tschanz was unable to follow what happened after Charnel's arrival. He fainted twice while the doctor from Neuveville bandaged his wounds; however, his injuries turned out to be harmless. Some villagers came later, peasants, workers, women. The courtyard was so crowded that the police had to bar the entrance. One young woman managed to push her way into the hall and threw herself screaming onto Gastmann's body. It was the waitress, Charnel's fiancée. He stood by, red with anger. Then Tschanz was carried to the car through the throng of retreating peasants.

"There they are, all three of them," Lutz said the next morning, with a gesture indicating the corpses, but his voice did not sound triumphant; it sounded sad and tired.

Von Schwendi nodded, dismayed. The colonel had driven to Biel with Lutz on his client's instructions.

They had come into the room where the bodies lay. A slanting shaft of light fell through a small barred window. The two men stood there in their coats and felt cold. Lutz had red eyes. He had spent the whole night reading Gastmann's journals, which were written in shorthand and difficult to decipher.

Lutz buried his hands deeper in his pockets. "That's how we are, von Schwendi," he began again, almost softly. "We're so scared of each other that we set up armed camps called states. We surround ourselves with guards of all sorts, with policemen, with soldiers, with public opinion; what good does it do?" Lutz twisted his face into a grimace, his eyes bulged, and he laughed. It came out as a hollow, goatish bleat in the cold, barren room. "A single dunce at the head of a world power, Councillor, and we'll be carried off by the floods. One Gastmann, and already our cordons are cut through, our outposts outflanked."

Von Schwendi realized it would be best to bring the examining magistrate back down to earth, but he didn't quite know how. "Exactly," he finally said. "Our circles are shamelessly exploited by all sorts of people. It's embarrassing, highly embarrassing."

"No one had any idea," Lutz said reassuringly.

"And Schmied?" asked the national councillor, glad to have found the key word.

"We found a folder in Gastmann's possession that had belonged to Schmied. It contained information about Gastmann's life and conjectures about his crimes. Schmied was trying to apprehend Gastmann.

He did this on his own private recognizance. An error for which he had to pay with his life; for we have proof that Schmied's murder was ordered by Gastmann: Schmied had to have been killed with the same weapon one of the servants was holding when Tschanz shot him. The examination of the weapon confirmed this immediately. The motive for the murder is also clear: Gastmann was afraid of being exposed by Schmied. Schmied should have confided in us. But he was young and ambitious."

Barlach came into the morgue. When Lutz saw the old man, he became melancholy and buried his hands in his pockets. "Well, Inspector," he said, shifting his weight from one foot to the other, "it's nice that we're meeting here. You have come back in time from your vacation, and I, too, have rushed over here with my state councillor and arrived in good time, as you see. There are the dead, served up for our delectation. We have had our quarrels, Barlach, many times. I was in favor of a super-sophisticated police force with all the latest paraphernalia, including the atom bomb if I could have had my way, and you, Inspector, wanted something more human, a sort of rural gendarmerie stocked with good-natured grandfathers. Let's bury the hatchet. We were both wrong. Tschanz refuted us by the very unscientific but straightforward use of his revolver. I don't want to know the details. Very well, it was self-defense, we have to believe him, and why shouldn't we. The catch was worth it, the men he shot deserved a thousand deaths, as they say, and if scientific method had prevailed, we would now be poking around in foreign affairs. I will have to promote Tschanz; while you and I, I'm afraid, are left looking like fools. The Schmied case is closed."

Lutz lowered his head, bewildered by the old man's enigmatic silence, and felt his proud posture collapsing into that of a proper, conscientious official. He cleared his throat and, noticing von Schwendi's embarrassment, blushed. Slowly, then, accompanied by the colonel, he walked out of the room and into the darkness of the hallway, leaving Barlach alone. The bodies lay on stretchers and were covered with black cloths. The plaster was peeling off the bare, gray walls. Barlach went to the middle stretcher and uncovered the body. It was Gastmann. Barlach bent over him slightly, holding the black cloth in his left hand. Silently he gazed into the waxen face of the dead man. There was still an amused expression on his lips. But his eyes were set even more deeply than in life, and there was no longer anything terrible lurking in those depths. Thus they met for the last time, the hunter and his prey, who now lay dead at his feet. Barlach sensed that both their lives were at an end now, and once again he looked back on the labyrinthine paths of their mysteriously intertwined lives. Now there remained nothing between them but the immensity of death, a judge whose verdict is silence. Barlach still stood slightly bent, and the pale light of the cell flickered and played equally on Barlach's face and hands and Gastmann's body, meant for both, created for both, reconciling them both. The silence of death sank down upon him, crept into him, but it gave him no peace as it had to the other man. The dead are always right. Slowly Barlach covered Gastmann's face with the cloth. This was the last time he would see him; from now on his enemy belonged to the grave. A single thought had obsessed him for years: to destroy the man who now lay at his feet in the cool gray room, covered with falling plaster as if with fine flakes of snow; and now there was nothing left for the old man but to wearily cover his enemy's face, and humbly beg for forgetfulness, the only mercy that can soothe a heart consumed by a raging fire.

20

That same evening, at eight o'clock sharp, Tschanz arrived at the old man's house in the Altenberg district. Barlach had urgently asked him to come at that hour. To his surprise, a young maid in a white apron opened the door, and as he stepped into the hallway, he heard the sounds of boiling water and roasting fat and the clatter of dishes. The maid removed the coat from his shoulders. His left arm was in a sling, but he had been able to come in his own car. The maid opened the door to the dining room, and Tschanz stopped in his tracks: the table was festively set for two people. Candles were burning in a candelabrum, and Barlach was sitting in an armchair at one end of the table, softly lit by the reddish light of the flames, the very image of imperturbable calm.

"Sit down, Tschanz," the old man called out to his guest, pointing at a second armchair that had been pulled up to the table. Tschanz sat down, stunned.

"I didn't know I was coming to dinner," he finally said.

"We have to celebrate your victory," the old man quietly replied, pushing the candelabrum a little to the side so that they could look each other fully in the face. Then he clapped his hands. The door opened, and a stately, rotund woman brought in a tray overflowing with sardines, lobster, a salad of cucumbers, tomatoes, and peas garnished with mountains of mayonnaise and eggs, and dishes with cold chicken, slices of cold roast, and salmon. Barlach helped himself to everything. Tschanz watched the man with the ailing stomach assemble a portion fit for a giant, and was so baffled he merely asked for a little potato salad.

"What shall we drink?" Barlach asked. "Ligerzer?"

"Ligerzer's fine with me," Tschanz replied as if dreaming. The maid came and filled their glasses. Barlach started to eat, helped himself to some bread, devoured the salmon, the sardines, the flesh of the red lobsters, the chicken, the salads, the mayonnaise, and the cold roast, clapped his hands, and asked for a second serving. Tschanz, who was still picking at his potato salad, looked petrified. Barlach called for a third glass of white wine.

"Let's have the pâtés and the red Neuenberger," he called out. The plates were changed. Barlach requested three pâtés, filled with goose liver, pork, and truffles.

"But you're sick, Inspector," Tschanz finally said, hesitantly.

"Not today, Tschanz, not today. This is a day for celebration. I've finally nailed Schmied's killer!"

He drained his second glass of red wine and started on his third pâté, eating without pause, stuffing himself with the world's good food, crushing each mouthful between his jaws like a demon attempting to still an unappeasable hunger. His body cast a shadow on the wall, twice his size, and the powerful movements of his arms and lowered head resembled the triumphal dance of an African chieftain. Appalled, Tschanz watched the terminally sick man's ghastly performance. He sat without moving, and was no longer eating or so much as touching his food. Nor did he once raise his glass to his lips. Barlach ordered veal cutlets, rice, French fries, green salad, and champagne. Tschanz was trembling.

"You're pretending," he said, with a choked voice. "You aren't sick at all!"

Barlach didn't answer immediately. At first he laughed, then he occupied himself with the salad, savoring each leaf, one by one. Tschanz did not dare ask the gruesome old man his question again.

"Yes, Tschanz," Barlach finally said, and his eyes flashed wildly, "I've been pretending. I was never sick." And he shoved a piece of veal into his mouth and continued eating, incessantly, insatiably.

And now Tschanz realized that he had walked into a cunningly prepared trap, and that the door was just now falling shut behind him. Cold sweat burst from his pores. Horror gripped him like a pair of mighty arms. His realization came too late, there was no way out.

"You know, Inspector," he said softly.

"Yes, Tschanz, I know," Barlach said calmly and firmly, without raising his voice, as though commenting on a matter of indifference. "You are Schmied's murderer." Then he reached for his glass of champagne and emptied it in one draft.

"I always had the feeling that you knew," Tschanz said almost inaudibly.

The old man's face remained expressionless. Nothing seemed to interest him more than this meal; relentlessly, he heaped a second mound of rice on his plate, poured gravy over it, topped it with a veal cutlet. Once again Tschanz tried to find an escape, a defense against this fiendish eater.

"The bullet came from the gun they found on the servant," he stated defiantly. But his voice sounded disheartened.

Barlach's narrowed eyes glittered with contempt. "Nonsense, Tschanz. You know perfectly well that that was *your* gun, and that you put it in the dead man's hand. Your only cover was the fact that Gastmann was found to be a criminal."

"You'll *never* be able to prove this," Tschanz desperately exclaimed.

The old man stretched in his seat, no longer sick and decrepit but powerful and relaxed, exuding a superiority that seemed almost godlike, a tiger playing with his victim. He drank the rest of his champagne. Then he stopped the waitress, who had been walking in and out, clearing the table and bringing more food, and asked her to bring some cheese, to which he added radishes, pearl onions, and pickled cucumbers. He consumed one delicacy after another, as if to taste one last time the good things of this earth.

"Do you really not realize, Tschanz," he finally said, "that you gave me the proof of your guilt long ago?

The gun was yours. You see, Gastmann's dog, which you shot in order to save me, had a bullet in his body that had to come from the same weapon that killed Schmied: *your* weapon. You yourself supplied me with the evidence I needed. You gave yourself away when you saved my life."

"When I saved your life! So that's why I couldn't find the dog when I went back," Tschanz replied mechanically. "Did you know that Gastmann had a bloodhound?"

"Yes. I had a blanket wrapped around my left arm."

"So that, too, was a trap," the murderer said with a toneless voice.

"That too. But the first proof you gave me was on Friday, when you insisted on driving to Ligerz via Ins so you could put on that farce about the 'blue Charon.' On Wednesday, Schmied drove through Zollikofen, not Ins. I knew this, because on that night, he stopped at the garage in Lyss."

"How could you know that?" Tschanz asked.

"I simply made a call. The man who drove through Ins and Erlach on that night was the murderer: you, Tschanz. You came from Grindelwald. The Pension Eiger also has a blue Mercedes. For weeks you had observed Schmied, watched his every step, jealous of his abilities, his success, his education, his girl. You knew he was investigating Gastmann, you even knew on what days he visited him, but you didn't know why. Then, by coincidence, the briefcase with the documents on his desk fell into your hands. You made a decision: to kill Schmied and take over the Gastmann case, so that you could for once enjoy some real success. It would be easy, you thought, to pin a murder on Gastmann, and you were right. So when I saw a blue Mercedes in Grindelwald, everything fell into place. You rented that car on Wednesday evening. I know you did, because I asked. The rest is simple: you drove to Schernelz through Ligerz and left the car standing in the woods near Twann. You crossed the forest by taking a short cut through the ravine, which took you to the Twann–Lamboing highway. You waited for Schmied by the cliffs, he recognized you, and stopped, surprised to see you there. He opened the door, and then you killed him. You told me so yourself. And now you have what you wanted: his success, his position, his car, and his girlfriend."

Tschanz listened to the merciless chess player who had checkmated him and was now finishing his horrible meal. The candles were wavering, their light flickered on the faces of the two men, the shadows were growing more dense. A deadly silence reigned in this nocturnal hell. The maids were no longer coming into the room. The old man sat motionless now, scarcely breathing, his face bathed in wave after wave of flickering light, a red fire that broke against the ice of his brow and his soul.

"You played with me," Tschanz said slowly.

"I played with you," Barlach replied with a terrible gravity. "I couldn't do otherwise. You took Schmied. I had to take you."

"In order to kill Gastmann," interjected Tschanz, suddenly realizing the whole truth.

"That's it. I gave up half my life to get Gastmann convicted, and Schmied was my last hope. I put him on the tracks of the devil incarnate, like setting a noble animal on the trail of some vicious beast. But then you came along, Tschanz, with your ridiculous, criminal ambition, and destroyed my only chance. So I took *you,* you, the killer, and turned you into my most terrible weapon. Because you were driven by desperation. The killer had to find another killer. I made my goal your goal."

"It was pure hell for me," Tschanz said.

"It was hell for both of us," the old man continued with terrible calmness. "Von Schwendi's interference pushed you over the edge, you had to somehow establish that Gastmann was the murderer, because every deviation from Gastmann's trail could lead to yours. Schmied's briefcase was the only thing that could help you. You knew it was in my possession, but you didn't know that Gastmann had taken it away. That's why you attacked me on Saturday night. Also, you didn't want me to go to Grindelwald."

"You knew it was I who attacked you?" Tschanz asked with a blank, toneless voice.

"I knew that from the very first moment. Everything I did was done with the intention of driving you to the utmost desperation. And when your despair reached the breaking point, you went to Lamboing to force a decision one way or another."

"One of Gastmann's servants fired the first shot," Tschanz said.

"I told Gastmann on Sunday morning that I was sending someone to kill him."

Tschanz reeled and felt himself turn cold as ice. "Then you pitted us both on each other, like animals!"

"Beast against beast," came the pitiless voice from the other chair.

"So you were the judge, and I was the hangman," Tschanz said, almost choking.

"That is correct," replied the old man.

"And I, who was only carrying out your will, whether I wanted to or not, I'm a criminal now, a man to be hunted!"

Tschanz stood up, leaning on the table with his uninjured right hand. Only one candle was still lit. With burning eyes Tschanz tried to make out the shape of the old man in the darkness, but all he could see was an unreal, black shadow. He made an uncertain, groping movement in the direction of his breast pocket.

"Don't do that," he heard the old man say. "It makes no sense. Lutz knows you are here with me, and the women are still in the house."

"You're right, it makes no sense," Tschanz replied softly.

"The Schmied case is settled," the old man said through the darkness of the room. "I won't betray you. But leave! Go anywhere! I don't want to see you ever again. It's enough that I judged *one* man. Go! Go!"

Tschanz lowered his head and walked out slowly, letting the door fall into the lock, and as he drove off, blending with the night, the candle went out, sputtering, and with a last sudden flare lit up the face of the old man, who had closed his eyes.

21

Barlach sat through the night in his armchair, without standing up once. The enormous, avid vitality that had flared up in him was collapsing and threatened to die altogether. The old man had taken one last, wildly audacious risk, but he had lied to Tschanz in one respect. When, at the break of dawn, Lutz came storming into his room to report with great consternation that Tschanz had been found dead in his car after being hit by a train between Twann and Ligerz, he found the inspector mortally ill. With an effort, the old man ordered him to remind Hungertobel that it was Tuesday, and that he was ready for the operation.

"Just one more year," Lutz heard the old man say as he stared through the window into the glassy morning. "Just one more year."

———

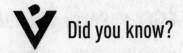

Did you know?

Swiss writer Friedrich Dürrenmatt was one of the most highly regarded German-language novelists and dramatists of the twentieth century, and his works have been translated into 49 languages. As a dramatist he wrote plays that reflected the mood of a war-scarred Europe. As a novelist, he is famed for his philosophical crime thrillers, which draw comparisons to the works of Paul Auster and Umberto Eco for their post-modern questioning of the conventions of the genre.

Dürrenmatt thought detective novels should reflect the absurdity of real life rather than proceeding like mathematical equations with a definite solution. Of the traditional crime writers, he once said, "You set up your stories logically, like a chess game: all the detective needs to know is the rules, he replays the moves of the game, and checkmate, the criminal is caught and justice has triumphed. This fantasy drives me crazy."

Dürrenmatt's most famous novel, *The Pledge*, was initially written as a screenplay titled *Es geschah am hellichten Tag* (*It Happened in Broad Daylight*). The film producers compelled Dürrenmatt to bring this original to a neat conclusion that they felt was more suitable for the screen. The decidedly unneat conclusion of the subsequent novel, and the subtitle *Requiem for the Detective Novel*, reflect Dürrenmatt's deep dislike of such formulaic and predictable plot constructions. Ironically, this book went on to spawn two successful movies, including a 2001 film starring Jack Nicholson and directed by Sean Penn.

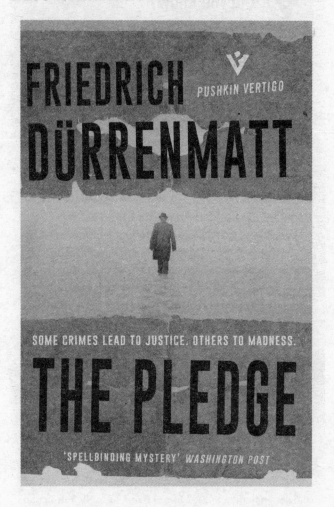

FRIEDRICH DÜRRENMATT

PUSHKIN VERTIGO

AN INSPECTOR BARLACH MYSTERY

SUSPICION

'SPELLBINDING' *WASHINGTON POST*